Praise for Tammy L. Grace,

author of The Hometown Harbor Series and the
Cooper Harrington Detective Novels

Killer Music (Book 1) is an award winning novel, earning the 2016 Mystery Gold Medal by the Global E-Book Awards

"Killer Music is a clever and well-crafted whodunit. The vivid and colorful characters shine as the author gradually reveals their hidden secrets—an absorbing page-turning read."
— *Jason Deas, bestselling author of Pushed and Birdsongs*

"I could not put this book down! It was so well written & a suspenseful read! This is definitely a 5 star story! I'm hoping there will be a sequel!"
—*Colleen, review of Killer Music*

Deadly Connection (Book 2) is an award winning novel, earning the 2017 Mystery Gold Medal by the Global E-Book Awards

"Wonderful book! I love Coop and AB, but I am totally head over heels with Gus the Golden Retriever! Having had Golden Retrievers, myself, Ms. Grace perfectly describes every perk of his ears and tail wag!! This was a great read and I had a hard time putting it down. Can't wait for another Cooper Harrington mystery!"
—*booklover.*

D0916656

Tammy L. Grace

Dead Wrong

A Cooper Harrington Detective Novel

Dead Wrong
A novel by
Tammy L. Grace

www.tammylgrace.com
Facebook: https://www.facebook.com/tammylgrace.books
Twitter: @TammyLGrace

Published in the United States by Lone Mountain Press, Nevada

ISBN 978-1-945591-05-1 (paperback)
ISBN 978-1-945591-06-8 (eBook)
FIRST EDITION

Cover design by Alchemy Book Covers and Design
Interior Formatting by Polgarus Studio
Printed in the United States of America

ALSO BY TAMMY L. GRACE

Cooper Harrington Detective Novels

Killer Music

Deadly Connection

Hometown Harbor Series

Hometown Harbor: The Beginning
(FREE Prequel Novella)

Finding Home

Home Blooms

A Promise of Home

Pieces of Home

Finally Home

For Zoe, the inspiration for Gus
and my loyal writing companion

Chapter 1

Myrtle slid a heaping platter of the breakfast special in front of Coop and added a short stack of pecan pancakes to Ben's side of the booth. "You boys eat up, now. It's cold outside." She refilled their coffee cups and stepped away to retrieve another order.

It was the first Friday breakfast of the new year. Coop and Ben occupied their favorite booth at Peg's Pancakes, where they had been meeting for the last two decades. The pair had met in college years ago and were closer than brothers.

Coop zipped his jacket over his t-shirt that read "Fitness Protection Program…I'm hiding from exercise" and shivered. "Usually I'm never cold, but after that tropical vacation, it does feel more than chilly today." He poured a wide ribbon of syrup atop his mound of fluffy pancakes.

"You're back to work Monday, right?" asked Ben.

Coop nodded as he speared a forkful into his mouth. "Yep, vacation's over."

He swallowed a sip of his favorite brew. "Gus will be glad to get back to normal. He was none too happy when we left him for two weeks."

"I'm sure he's been milking it now," said Ben, with a smile. "That dog has all of us trained."

Coop lips curved into a slow smile. "You know him well." He

glanced out the window and saw Gus staring back at him from the passenger seat of the Jeep. "AB and I are going to work for a few hours this morning, just to get a semblance of order established in the office before Monday."

Coop slid a bag across the table. "Almost forgot. Got you a little something from the Bahamas."

Ben opened the bag and pulled out a baseball cap with a bright floral brim. Ben always wore baseball caps when he wasn't working. Some speculated it was to cover his balding head. Coop grinned and said, "Figured you could add another to your collection."

"Nice one. Although in this weather, I need a knitted cap."

"I tried to find one. Those are difficult to come by in the tropics."

"Did you get caught up on all the news or read the papers from when you were gone yet?"

Coop shook his head. "No, I need to do that today and tomorrow. I've been playing with Gus and doing some laundry. Took a few naps yesterday after we put all the Christmas decorations away. Aunt Camille never remembers how much she has until it's time to store it."

"Knowing her, she probably still buys more each year." Ben took a long sip from his cup. "You and AB are still coming over tomorrow, right? Jen's been cooking up a storm."

"Yeah, yeah. It'll be fun. We were happy Jen decided to postpone the party until we returned. We know how much she always likes throwing her New Year's Eve party."

"She talked me into a fancy fire pit for the backyard, so she's hoping the weather stays dry so we can enjoy it tomorrow night. The kids have dozens of bags of marshmallows to roast. Hopefully, I won't get called out like I usually do on New Year's Eve. Should be a calmer evening."

"Don't jinx it." Coop grinned and continued to work his way through breakfast. "So, anything exciting happen?"

"Well, it's always something. We had a home invasion with the intruders killed by the homeowner and our regular holiday crime sprees. The hoodlums seem to multiply during the season of giving."

"Chalk one up for the homeowner. I like it when the good guys win. Sounds like that kept you busy."

Ben nodded. "Oh, you remember Chandler Hollund from Vanderbilt?"

Coop's brow furrowed. "Yeah, he was set on being a doctor or researcher or something, right?"

"That's him. He's a partner in that big pharmaceutical company that moved into that new technology campus off West End Avenue a few years ago. It's called Borlund Sciences."

Coop nodded. "Yeah, I remember reading about it. Sounds like he's done well for himself. Always was a brainiac-type. Way too smart to go to law school." Coop laughed and took another swig of coffee when he saw Myrtle coming with a fresh pot.

"His partner, Neil Borden, died late last week. Collapsed in their private dining room at their headquarters."

"Chandler's our age. Pretty young to be dead."

Ben's head bobbed in agreement. "Borden was a couple of years older, but not much. Doc said it was a massive brain bleed. Borden was the business guru of their company. No medical background."

Coop eyed his plate as he swept a piece of pancake across it to pick up the last traces of egg and bacon. He set his fork down. "I should quit eating all this fat and cholesterol. I always think I'll cut back when I'm older, but hearing that makes me reconsider."

"This guy looked healthy. One of those fanatics who ran and worked out. Watched what he ate. Probably wore the same size pants he did in college."

Coop grimaced. "That doesn't make me feel any better."

Myrtle interrupted when she placed a container on the table and added the check on top. "Tell AB howdy from me. Y'all have a good weekend." She turned and added, "I'm glad y'all are back home."

Coop dug into his pocket for his wallet. "We had fun but are glad to be back in Nashville. Gus missed us." He stacked bills on top of the check and said, "See ya next week."

They slid out of the booth. Coop, tall and lanky, with a thick head of dark hair, just beginning to gray, was a stark contrast to Ben. Nashville's Chief of Detectives was short and stocky, hanging on to his thinning ashy blonde hair, but losing the battle. Ben followed Coop outside and gave Gus a good neck rub. "You keep your eye on Coop today. Don't let him slack off."

Gus gave Ben a grin, and the tip of his tongue fell out of his mouth signaling his approval of the massage. Coop gave Ben a wave and sped off for his office. Gus was back in his routine and bounded up the back steps, waiting for Coop to open the door.

The dog vaulted through the kitchen and into the front of the house that served as the office of Harrington and Associates. Coop smelled the familiar aroma of his favorite decaffeinated coffee brewing. AB was busy opening mail and sorting it into piles.

Coop added her takeout box to the mess on her desk. "Breakfast is served."

"Oh, thanks. Smells delicious. I left you a stack of messages on your desk. Sounds like a couple of new jobs in the mix." She opened the box and gazed at her scramble and pancakes. Gus scooted himself under her desk, positioning his mouth atop her thigh and waited.

She took a few bites and slipped him one, while she sorted through the papers strewn across her desk. Coop left them to eat and started a fire in the fireplace before going through his mail and messages.

By noon AB's desk was almost clean, and Coop had returned all but a few calls. The house was warm and bustling, as it had been when Coop and AB had worked for Uncle John when they were attending Vanderbilt. They had spent many happy hours in the office, learning at the side of Coop's capable uncle.

Coop loved the fact that Uncle John and Aunt Camille had trusted him with the business after his uncle's death. He warmed his hands in front of the fire and ran his palm along the wooden desk that had belonged to his uncle. He felt at home here, but the sight of Uncle John's empty chair tugged at his heart.

AB came through his door, flipping her hair over the top of her collar. Coop noticed her blondish hair had lightened from their time in the sun. He suspected she colored it since at times it seemed blonder and other times had a reddish blonde tone. He was smart enough never to inquire about her hair color. She finished adjusting her coat and said, "I'm gonna take off. I need to run to the store and get a few things for the party tomorrow."

"Sounds good. Gus and I will pick you up around three. No sense in taking two cars."

"I'll meet you here. That will save you time. Did Camille decide to come?"

"Nah, she's going to some classic movie night with a couple of friends."

"That sounds fun and more her speed."

Coop laughed in agreement and said, "I'll be here for a couple of hours before I pick you up. I want to get all this," he gestured to his desk, "organized and ready for Monday."

"I'll give you two weeks tops before this place looks like a disaster again. Your resolve to keep your desk clean usually wears off before the end of January." Her blue-green eyes danced with amusement. She gave him a wink and waved goodbye.

Gus stared at Coop from his perch on the leather chair. "Yeah, I know she's right, but it wouldn't be the start of a new year without a resolution."

* * *

Coop was enjoying the banter and conversation around the new fire pit. Ben's kids plus a couple of their friends were handing out sticks for marshmallows. Gus was busy herding the kids around and swiping a few marshmallows from their sticky fingers.

Rather than a fancy party, Jen had made a huge spread of appetizers, chili, and soups. A couple of officers were regaling the group with a story about one of their more colorful arrests over the holidays while Jen delivered plates of dessert to the guests.

Coop felt his cell phone vibrate in his pocket and plucked it out to read the screen. It was a call transferred from the after-hours number at the office. He drifted away from the group, and Gus stayed with AB. The air was nippy away from the comfort of the fire, but he wanted to avoid the chatter in the background and stepped to the edge of the yard.

"Harrington and Associates," he said in his most professional voice.

"Cooper, is that you?"

"Yes, this is Cooper Harrington, who is this?"

"It's Chandler Hollund. From Vanderbilt. Not sure if you remember me."

"Ah, yes, I remember. It's been a long time. What can I do for you?"

"I'm sorry to call so late and on the weekend. I was trying to wait until Monday to contact you. I left you a voicemail earlier this afternoon and then thought more about it and decided to use your emergency number."

"That's okay, what is it I can do for you?"

"I'm in trouble. Big trouble. I need to see you as soon as possible."

Coop recalled Ben telling him about Chandler's business partner. "Well, I can meet you tomorrow—"

Chandler interrupted, "Is there any way we could talk tonight? I'm concerned I may be arrested soon."

"Uh, okay. I can be at my office in about thirty minutes." He wandered back over to the group as he disconnected the call.

He squeezed into the circle of guests next to AB and whispered, "Client emergency. We need to get back to the office for a quick consult. Unless you want to stay and I could come back for you."

"No, I'll go. I was getting ready to ask you to leave anyway." They wished everyone a good evening and thanked Ben and Jen, taking a bag of leftovers she had packaged.

"It was all delicious. Thanks for this," said Coop, holding up the bag and hugging Jen. "Happy New Year."

They loaded into the Jeep and hurried to the office. He turned up the heat and flicked on a lamp in the reception area. Gus followed AB into the kitchen where she stored their provisions from Jen in the fridge and brewed a pot of tea.

Coop had positioned another log on the fire when he heard movement in the reception area, followed by the click of toenails on the wood as Gus scurried to the door. He heard AB say, "Come on in. Coop's in his office."

Coop made his way to the front door. As he arrived, he heard the man standing in front of AB say, "I can't tell you how much I appreciate him seeing me tonight. I'm sorry to be here so late. Are you Cooper's wife?"

She grinned and said, "Uh, no. I'm his assistant."

"Hey, Chandler," he said. "Ben was just telling me about your partner's death yesterday." He moved the door and opened it wider. "Welcome to my office. You remember Annabelle? She runs the place."

Chandler looked at AB and pursed his lips. "You look familiar, but I couldn't say for sure I remember you. I'm sorry and sorry for assuming you were his wife. I didn't expect anyone to be here."

She shook his extended hand. "Not to worry, Chandler. I think we had only a couple of classes together and it was a long time ago. You can call me AB, everybody does. How about a cup of coffee or tea?"

"Tea sounds great, AB," he said with a nervous grin.

"AB and I were at a get-together with friends tonight when you called." Coop led him into the office and herded Gus out of the way. Gus hopped into the leather chair he had commandeered as his years ago. "Have a seat, Chandler. What can we do for you?"

He ran his fingers through his thinning hair. "Where to begin with this nightmare?" His hands trembled as he steadied himself into the chair in front of Coop's desk. "You mentioned Ben told you about Neil's death. Two detectives visited me this morning. They asked a bunch of questions about my whereabouts and our partnership. They said his death is now a homicide investigation. It's making me uneasy. I've got a corporate attorney, and he referred me to a criminal attorney. I think they're going to arrest me for killing Neil."

He gripped his mug of tea and stared across the table at Coop. "I remember you, so when my lawyer suggested an investigator, I knew I had to speak with you. You have an excellent reputation for solving difficult cases, and you were the first detective my lawyer recommended. I need your help. I have to find out who killed Neil. Because it wasn't me."

"Okay, Chandler, let's slow down a minute and go through this. Do you have the names of the detectives that came to see you this morning?"

Chandler set his mug down and reached inside his jacket. He

retrieved two business cards and slipped them across the desk. He added a third card and said, "This is the lawyer I've retained."

Coop nodded as he read the lawyer's card and then picked up the other two cards bearing the official badge from Ben's division. "These two work for Ben Mason. Have you talked to Ben?"

Chandler shook his head. "No, just the detectives. I talked to the officers who arrived that day and the paramedics, but now things are different. We all thought Neil had a heart attack or stroke. Tragic, but not murder. Now, it seems something in the toxicology has come back indicating he had an excessive amount of a drug in his system." He shook his head. "I even helped them identify the drug. It's from our company, CX-232."

"My best advice is to let your criminal lawyer do the talking for you. Don't meet with the detectives without your lawyer and refer all questions to him." Coop fingered the business card. "Cal is top notch. He'll handle it like a pro."

Chandler swallowed hard and took a sip of tea. "I understand about letting him do all the talking. Cal said the same thing. Told me not to worry." He shook his head.

"I know that's hard to do, but let's focus on figuring this out." Coop drew a heavy line on his notepad. "Now, what is CX-232?"

Chandler's demeanor changed as he slipped into the role of a scientist describing the drug, CX-232, which he had developed. He explained it was designed to treat Alzheimer's. He became more animated as he took a pen and drew on one of Coop's pads, showing him how the drug disrupted the sticky proteins that formed plaque in the brain. Coop was lost in all the science-speak but appreciated how passionate Chandler was about his research and the ability to produce a treatment for a horrid disease.

Chandler rattled off all sorts of data and did his best to explain how the drug worked to interrupt the ability of specific proteins to clump and stick together. His eyes sparkled with enthusiasm as he illustrated the tangles, proteins, and peptides associated with the disease. When he finished, Chandler slid back into his chair and took a long swallow from his mug.

"That sounds like some exciting work. You seem confident it works. How many people were working on this with you?"

"I have a small team. There are just the six of us and Neil. We are just getting things together for the first trial in humans."

Coop made a note and said, "Let's start at the beginning. Tell me what happened when Neil died and in the days leading up to his death."

Coop spent the next three hours listening to Chandler and asking questions, jotting notes on his pad. Gus fell asleep. Coop caught his own eyes threatening to close due to the warmth of the fire and Chandler's quiet, and at times, monotone delivery.

Coop called an end to the interview. He had Chandler sign the contract AB had prepared for him while Chandler had recounted his conversation with the detectives. Chandler removed an envelope from his jacket pocket and handed it to Coop. "I hope that's enough to get you started. If not, let me know, and I'll send a messenger over with another one."

Coop moved the flap and took a look. "That's more than enough. Let's see where this leads and we'll send you an accounting at the end of the month."

"I can't tell you how much I appreciate this, Coop." Chandler stood and walked to the door with his old classmate.

"I'll see what I can find out from the detectives on the case, and we'll go from there. I'm hoping you misinterpreted their seriousness, but I'll talk to you Monday and see what we can figure out." Coop gave Chandler's shoulder a squeeze and locked the door behind him.

He turned and saw a sticky note on the corner of AB's otherwise immaculate desk. She had gone home but wanted to know the scoop and suggested they meet at the office on Sunday.

Coop roused Gus from his slumber. "Come on buddy; it's already tomorrow."

Chapter 2

Aunt Camille was sleeping in after a late night movie marathon. Coop, intent on letting her rest, skipped breakfast and ushered Gus to the Jeep. He stopped at the Donut Hole for a bag to go and started a pot of coffee brewing. Ben always joked with Coop, suggesting he would have made an excellent police officer with his fondness for donuts and coffee.

There were still a few embers in the fireplace. He coaxed them into igniting some newspaper and soon had flames licking a dry log. He tackled his desk, scanning pages, making piles for filing, shredding a few, and leaving others for further action.

Close to noon AB sent a text to let Coop know she was delayed and would be there later. Once he had his desktop cleared, except for a small stack of working files, he opened the drawers on his credenza.

He shook his head. "Whoa, that's a gigantic mess." He dug into the mounds of paperwork that had been stuffed into every available inch. He amassed a pile of junk mail, catalogs, and expired offers to toss, and went about filing the remaining correspondence.

Gus rocketed across the floor, and Coop heard the back door open a few minutes later. AB poked her head into his office and said, "Wow, you've been a busy bee. Sorry, I'm late. I'm going to start on the dusting and vacuuming."

Gus was no fan of the vacuum. He dove for his chair, and Coop shut the door while the whir of the machine droned throughout the old house. As Coop was hefting the pile of trash into a bag, he noticed the glow of the exterior Christmas lights. He had Taylor, a young man he met through one of his cases, install the lights before the holidays and had forgotten about them.

He groaned at the thought of taking them down. He heard the hum of the vacuum stop and Gus vacated his chair. Coop opened the door, and Gus darted out to sit by the other fireplace. It was a longstanding ritual. The dog knew AB and the intimidating sucking machine would be coming to Coop's office and he wanted to be somewhere else.

"I love the Christmas lights," she said, moving the powerhead through the door. "I vote we leave them for a couple of weeks so we can enjoy them. Since we were gone, we missed out on the fun."

"Works for me. I was dreading the thought of climbing around to take them down."

"I'll call Taylor and ask him to come on a nice day later in the month."

"Yeah, tell him no rush. Wait for a dry and warmer day." He lugged the bag of trash out and when he returned AB was wrapping up the cord of the vacuum.

When they finished the housekeeping chores and got the office back into shape for the coming week, it was time to head to Aunt Camille's. Mrs. Henderson was making a special meal to celebrate their return. Camille had invited AB to join them. Knowing Aunt Camille would be interested in their new case, and rather than have Coop repeat the whole story, AB suggested he wait until they were all together to share the details of Chandler's situation.

Camille's housekeeper prepared all the meals, except for Sundays. Aunt Camille had been making supper on Sundays for as long as

Coop could remember and she enjoyed the ritual. Tonight Mrs. Henderson was cooking a lavish meal to welcome them home from their holiday trip and give Camille a reprieve from cooking. Aunt Camille couldn't resist lending a hand and told Mrs. Henderson she could handle the last minute details.

When Coop and AB arrived, Aunt Camille was flicking hot biscuits off a baking sheet into a basket. "Yowza, that's hot." She glanced up and saw Coop. "Oh, good. I was getting worried about y'all. Supper's ready and I don't want it to get cold."

Gus rubbed up against Camille and pressed his head into her leg. "Get on your bed, Gus. Get out of the way," said Coop, grabbing a towel and holding the baking sheet for her.

He managed to get all the biscuits off, and AB helped carry serving dishes to the table. They sat down and over a hearty meal of meatloaf and mashed potatoes, Coop shared Chandler's conversation. "This is confidential, Aunt Camille, so don't share this with anyone. We're just getting started on this new case."

Her eyes twinkled as she shook her head causing feathery wisps of her white hair to bounce. "I know. I'll keep it to myself." She urged him on by attempting to raise the eyebrows she had penciled on her forehead that morning.

"A man we went to undergrad with at Vanderbilt, Chandler Hollund, hired us today. He wants us to find out who killed his partner, Neil Borden."

Camille waved her hand and took a sip of water to swallow. "Oh, yes, I saw in the paper that he had died at their offices. They made it sound like a heart attack, but he was murdered?"

"That's what Chandler thinks. Neil died from a massive brain bleed. The detectives paid him a visit yesterday morning and told him Borden had been drugged. Chandler's convinced they're going to arrest him."

"What makes him so sure?" asked AB.

"They told him he was a person of interest and not to leave the country. They asked for his passport, which he volunteered. They told him Borden's tox results were abnormal and upon further testing showed he had ingested a large quantity of a unique compound that is currently in development at Borlund. It's called CX-232, and it's for Alzheimer's. It's not on the market yet. Just in the early phase of the first human trial. He even helped them identify the drug as his."

"Eww, that doesn't sound good for Chandler," said AB.

Coop's head bobbed in agreement. "They also told him they had information that he and Neil had been fighting about the business and their relationship had been tense the last few months. Neil wanted to sell the company, and Chandler didn't. They had argued over that and the direction of the company. Chandler is a true researcher, not attuned to the business side and focused on the science and benefits of the drugs they develop. Neil Borden was all about the money."

"Oh, my. Sounds like a real mess," said Camille.

"Not to mention Chandler is the beneficiary of a large life insurance policy on Neil. They each had insurance on the other."

"How large?" asked AB.

"A hundred million."

AB choked on her drink. "Wow, that's a motive with a neon arrow pointing straight at him."

Camille pushed the bowl of potatoes closer to AB. "He sounds like a decent young man. Working to treat Alzheimer's and all. That's a dreadful disease. You know my friend, Dottie Mae?" She didn't wait for an answer. "Her husband has it. She's worn herself to a frazzle trying to care for him. I've been trying to convince her to get some help." She turned her attention back to Coop. "Do you believe your classmate?"

Coop frowned and said, "Yeah, I do. He's a straight shooter and didn't appear to be lying. I don't think he did anything, but he's as nervous as a long-tailed cat in a rocking chair factory."

"Does he have a guess at who would have wanted to kill Borden?" asked AB.

Coop shook his head. "No clue. He said he wasn't aware of any personal problems, but admitted they didn't socialize. Chandler is a nerd. He's always been that way. He's a loner and very focused on his work. A bit awkward in social settings."

"Does he have an alibi?" asked Camille.

Coop sucked in his breath. "The opposite, I'm afraid. He and Neil were having lunch in their private dining room. Neil invited him to have another conversation about selling to see if they could work out an agreement. Chandler ate his soup and then got upset and left. He was on his way back to his office on the other side of the building when they called him and told him Neil had collapsed."

Coop took a few bites and continued. "The medical examiner says the drug was most likely mixed with his food as she found significant concentrations of it and the soup in the stomach contents. CX-232 is an injectable, and after the incident, the team did an inventory. No vials are unaccounted for, but several of them have minute amounts missing.

"So the killer used a syringe and sucked out tiny bits from several vials to get enough to kill someone?

Coop nodded. "No fingerprints on the vials, since they all wear gloves when handling them anyway. That leaves the seven members of the team and the police cleared the rest of them."

"No wonder he's a suspect. He has the motive, means, and opportunity. Who else could it be?" asked AB.

Camille grinned. "Coop will figure it out. If he believes Chandler, he has to find the real killer." She started stacking empty plates. "How about some fresh pecan pie and ice cream?"

* * *

As Coop sat staring at his home office computer while he should have been sleeping, he reflected on the fact that he had slept much better in the Bahamas than he did anywhere else. He opened a new window on the screen and perused the selection of oceans sounds he could download, with the hope one of them would deliver a full night's sleep. He had battled insomnia for the last twenty years. It started in college around the time his mother informed his father she didn't love him and was leaving. She had bounced from man to man and had been a vagabond ever since.

He resisted medications, which all the doctors offered. He had tried sound machines and white noise, aromatherapy, essential oils, massage, acupuncture, special pillows and mattresses, blindfolds, earplugs, and blackout blinds. None had provided the solution. Except for the Bahamas. Their cottage had been right on the water and Coop thought it must have been the gentle sounds of the waves on the beach that provided the rest he craved. AB pointed out it could have been the tropical cocktails their group enjoyed each night.

He clicked a few audio files to sample while he thought about what he had learned while digging into the life of Chandler's partner. Borden was divorced and had no children. His ex-wife had remarried long ago and lived near Seattle. Borden was from California and had moved to Nashville when the business started. He made a note on his pad to ask Chandler how they had met.

He wrote down the word "money" on his notepad and circled it. He needed to take a look at the financial health of Borlund Sciences and look for a motive related to money. He scribbled a few more items on his list and turned his attention to his phone. He used it to find the audio file he liked best and went back to his bedroom where Gus was sound asleep.

Coop put the phone on his nightstand and shut his eyes, listening to the rhythm of the ocean slap the beach. Soon the thoughts of Neil Borden evaporated into much-needed sleep.

* * *

Coop texted Ben after a grueling workout at the gym Monday morning. Coop picked up another quick breakfast at the Donut Hole and started a fire to take the chill off the office. Ben arrived soon after and they huddled around the warmth while Coop explained Chandler had retained his services.

"I don't think he did it, Ben. Do you?"

"The evidence is circumstantial at this point, but it doesn't look good for him."

"I don't think he has it in him. He's a bookworm and a gentle guy. I can't imagine him getting mad enough to kill someone. He strikes me as a passive man. A lot like I remember him from college. His sole focus in life is science."

Ben popped another sugared bit of dough into his mouth. "That may be, but people snap. From what's in the report, it's a well-known fact the two of them had been fighting and arguing for months."

"Why would a smart cookie like Chandler kill his partner with a drug that can be tied back to him? If he snapped, wouldn't he just shove him out the window or run him over or something like that? This sounds like a planned poisoning."

"A hundred million bucks is a pretty good motive."

Coop scrunched his nose. "On the surface, maybe. It was a policy to protect each of them so that the business wouldn't suffer and they wouldn't have to make changes. They purchased the policies when they started the business and increased them as the business grew."

"You sound determined to find an alternative killer."

Coop nodded. "Yeah, something's not right. I need to look into it more, but I think he's innocent."

"I'll admit, we don't have a smoking gun, but he's one of the very few with access to that drug. The detectives cleared the rest of them."

"How long do you think we have before the DA charges him?"

"We haven't turned it over yet. I would say a few weeks."

"I would never ask you to procrastinate. I just really don't think he did it."

"I won't interfere, but happy to share what we know. I'll send you the case file. If we missed something, I'm all ears. I want to get the right guy, not just the most convenient one. At this point, I don't have anything else to go on. It'll be up to the DA if he wants to pursue something on a circumstantial case." Ben stood and took another pastry. "I've gotta get going."

"Thanks, Ben. I appreciate the cooperation. I'll keep you in the loop."

* * *

By the time AB arrived, the office was warm and filled with the inviting smell of coffee and a hint of deep-fried dough. Gus greeted AB and followed her to her desk. Once she was settled and poured herself a cup, she wandered into Coop's office.

He was standing at the whiteboard scribbling names and notes. "Ben sent over the case file, so I'm making a list of the people who worked at Borlund with access to this CX-232."

She watched as he finished adding the name Miller to his list of Hollund, Borden, McCutcheon, Harris, Swenson, and Devi. "So those seven people are the only ones with access to the area where the drug is made or stored?"

Coop nodded. "Ben's detectives talked to all of them and eliminated them, but I'm going to interview them again. These are the five scientists that work with Chandler and Neil on the CX-232 team. That's it. A small group out of the thousands of employees."

"Is it key card controlled?"

"Yep. I have copies of the file of all the activity in the lab. Each drug is confined to only one lab. There is no cross-over among the scientific teams. The only people who have swiped their card for that lab are these seven people."

"No janitors, repair people, guests, security?"

"All of those people are logged into the lab logs, but none are given cards. One of the team members must be present when a guest is in the lab. I'll have you start digging into the guest logs and set up interviews. I'm going to head over to Borlund this morning and see Chandler and start interviewing this group." He pointed to the names on the whiteboard.

"I'll need you to start running backgrounds on Borden and Chandler, along with the five scientists on his team. We need to see if there's something there that was missed."

"What about security? They always have keys to everything."

"They do have a master card that lets them in all the doors, but they're not permitted inside the laboratories unless there's an emergency. There's no record of them in there for months."

"Who else could have gotten their hands on that drug?"

"I was going to ask Chandler if anybody in the FDA or some other watchdog group would have been given a sample or anything like that. I can't figure it out."

She took the file from Coop and raised her brows at his t-shirt choice of the day. "Sarcasm...the body's natural defense against stupidity" was stenciled across Coop's torso. AB rolled her eyes and pointed at his chest. "Don't forget to change your shirt."

Chapter 3

Coop slipped one of his Harrington and Associates polo shirts on and made sure the collar was down before patting Gus on the head and hollering out a farewell to AB. Borlund Sciences was only a couple of miles away from the office. He elected not to call ahead. He would observe Chandler and get a look at the operation and his office without giving him time to prepare.

The lobby was one of those minimalistic modern spaces with stylish but uncomfortable furnishings. He approached the curved reception area and was greeted by a security guard. Coop explained he was working for Chandler Hollund and wished to see him.

The guard made a phone call and within a few minutes gave him a visitor badge and escorted him to a bank of elevators. The guard retrieved his card and swiped it against the panel inside the elevator and poked the button for the fifth floor. The elevator ride was quick, and the door opened to another small lobby.

The guard waved to the open door. Coop exited and nodded to the woman behind the futuristic white curved workspace. "You must be Mr. Harrington," said the woman. "Mr. Hollund is waiting in his office."

She stood and came around the desk to greet Coop. "I'm Amanda, Mr. Hollund's assistant. Please follow me."

She directed Coop to a generous corner office where Chandler was waiting. She offered beverages and Coop opted for water. Chandler welcomed Coop to a chair at a glass conference table with a view from the top floor of the building.

Coop didn't waste time with small talk. "I talked to Ben and have the police file. I need to interview your team and anyone else who had access to the lab where the drug was developed and stored. I'd also like their personnel files so we can run complete backgrounds on all of them."

Chandler nodded in small bursts. "Sure, we can set that up. I'll have Amanda schedule you in the conference room here on this floor. I don't think any of them would do anything to harm Neil, but Amanda can provide you copies from their files."

"I understand. I'm being thorough. I'd also like to get a look at the dining room and the kitchen operations. I want to trace the food chain, so to speak."

"Excellent. I'll have Amanda get a security officer to accompany you and take you wherever you want to go in the building. If you need access to any of the laboratories, you'll just need to sign in on the lab log."

"As I understand it, CX-232 was produced and stored in only the one lab, right?"

"Yes, we make sure each drug in production or development has its own lab. That eliminates all cross-contamination possibilities along with the security and ownership for the team. They know their work files and notes are secure and won't be accessed by anyone other than authorized team members."

"Is there any way to override the security access system? Do you have someone on staff that manages it and controls it?"

"The security department manages it via computer, but as far as repairs or problems we have a contract with the manufacturer. Security could tell you the last time they were here for a repair problem and can produce any records you need. Any overrides or bypass of the card reader would be logged in the system. It would normally be for someone who forgot their card or something like that. We have strict protocols to verify an identity and any non-card access is documented and reviewed. It's rare."

"The detective cleared your team, which leaves you with the only motive. I'm trying to figure out if we're missing someone who would have had access to the drug."

Chandler took a sip from his coffee cup. "I understand. I've been trying to piece it together myself. I can't think of a way."

"Keep thinking. We're missing something." Coop stood and made his way to the door. "I'll come back by on my way out."

Amanda arranged for the scientists on Chandler's team to meet Coop in a well-appointed conference room and made sure it was stocked with snacks and arranged for lunch to be delivered. Coop adjusted the high-tech chair, took out a notepad and pen, and waited for his first interviewee to arrive.

The door opened, and an attractive woman with dark hair and skin the color of caramel introduced herself. "I'm Kanti Devi," she said, extending her hand.

Coop motioned to a chair and thanked her for coming. "I'm investigating the death of Neil Borden, and I know you've already spoken with the police. I'm going over everything and working for Mr. Hollund to find Mr. Borden's killer."

"I understand. I can't believe anyone would think Dr. Hollund could kill Mr. Borden. He is a kind and gentle person. Very intelligent and very committed to his work and the company. It is all so distressing. How can I help?"

Coop went through a litany of questions he had composed at the office. He wanted to tease out any information the team had about each of the partners, CX-232, the security of the laboratory, and their thoughts about who would have wanted to kill Mr. Borden.

He also asked the team members to tell him about their training and work on the team. They all possessed degrees that earned them the title of doctor. "Dr. Devi, is there anyone outside of the team members who would have access to CX-232?"

She shook her head. "No. It's all secure in the laboratory. We were just setting up a patient room to begin our trials."

"So, no drugs had been dispensed yet?"

"No, we had completed our animal studies and received approval to move forward with the next phase." Dr. Devi explained her primary role had been in the development of CX-232 and now she was transitioning to assist with the monitoring and tracking of the results from trials with the hope of results that would gain FDA approval.

Coop probed each scientist and learned from Dr. Miller, the team member in charge of the animal studies, that the animals had been housed in the secure lab and the CX-232 did not leave the lab during any of the procedures. The drug was administered to a number of rodents who were tracked throughout the experimental period.

Next to meet Coop was Dr. Phyllis Swenson. "We were so excited to get approval to move forward with Phase 1 trials on humans. We have a hundred people lined up to begin the treatment next month. We were working on all the preparations for administering and tracking the results. That's my main focus now, coordinating the trial."

When Dr. Swenson left, Amanda opened the door and directed staff to set up the lunch offerings on a table in the back of the room. She handed Coop a neat stack of papers enclosed in a thick envelope. "Here are the copies you requested. Security also made you a copy of the camera footage for the day and some of the door access logs.

It's the same information they provided to the police."

Coop thanked her and fixed himself a plate of food while he waited for Dr. Harris to arrive. He was surprised at the quality of the food. The soup tasted homemade. The salad was fresh and full of a variety of colorful vegetables. Another tray held a selection of bread, meats, and cheeses, plus everything he could think of to add to a sandwich. Frosted brownies and soft cookies topped off the buffet.

Amanda checked on Coop and went about making herself a plate. "You've got about thirty minutes to eat before your next appointment. Chandler will be by in a few minutes to join you for lunch."

"This is all delicious. I'm shocked that a company cafeteria has such tasty food."

"They do a great job. It's not some big food service provider. They're all employees of Borlund and provide homemade food. It was important to Mr. Borden and Mr. Hollund to create an environment that eliminated typical employee worries. We have childcare, the cafeteria, which will also prepare take-home dinners, a huge gym with a swimming pool and sauna, and lots of other amenities. It's all free, except the takeout dinners."

"Employees love it here; they're happy and productive. It helps them cope with the long hours that are sometimes required," she finished fixing her plate and walked toward the door.

"Please have a seat. I'd like to pick your brain for a few minutes," said Coop, pulling out a chair.

She smiled and set her plate on the table. "What do you want to know?"

"Tell me about Neil and Chandler. How did their relationship work?"

"I've been here since the beginning, and it all seemed great until a few months ago. Neil found a buyer for the company and wanted to sell. Chandler didn't. Money doesn't mean much to Chandler. He wanted to keep working on the research and development. He thinks CX-232 is very promising and has a lot of faith in it."

"Why did Neil want to sell?"

She shook her head as she swallowed. "I'm not sure. I know Chandler was going to see if there was a way to buy him out or find another partner, rather than sell. He tried to convince Neil that once the drug had gone through the trials, they would be able to make even more money, but Neil was adamant about selling now."

"I take it Neil had his own assistant?"

"Yeah, Melissa Schwarz is his assistant. I can introduce you."

Chandler walked in and waved a greeting before filling a plate. He took a seat on the other side of Coop. "How's it going?"

Coop nodded and gestured to Amanda. "I've just been given the copies of the files, will finish up the interviews this afternoon, and Amanda said she'd introduce me to Neil's assistant." He wiped his mouth with a napkin and added, "I'll come back tomorrow for the kitchen tour."

Amanda excused herself and reminded Coop of his appointment time.

"Tell me how your employees are vetted before they're hired. In particular, the support staffers like those in the kitchen and janitorial services."

Chandler explained he had limited knowledge of that area, as Neil had handled all the administrative minutia, but he knew the security department was involved. They had never had any issues with pilfering. "We also don't tolerate poor performance or problems. We don't have much turnover. We pay well and have good benefits for all of our employees."

Coop made a note and finished his brownie. "I haven't picked up on anything that raised concerns from my interviews. I'll know more in the coming days. You're continuing to move forward with the human trial?"

Chandler nodded. "Yes, we reported the situation of Neil's death. They agreed there's nothing about it to indicate an issue with CX-232. It wasn't applied in the normal dosage, so the resulting death is not attributable to the drug. We're planning to move forward."

"Have you heard from the buyer who was interested in acquiring the company?"

"Not yet. Melissa may know more about that. I'm going to have to find another business partner since my focus is on the science. I stayed out of the other side of things." Chandler stood and collected his plate and silverware. "I'll let you get back to it. Talk to you tomorrow."

As soon as he left, Coop snagged a couple of bottles of iced tea from the tub of drinks. He took a sip before Dr. McCutcheon came through the door. The young man shook hands with Coop and smiled. "Call me Mac, everybody does." He began by explaining his role on the team. As Coop listened to him outline his training and education in computer sciences and mathematics, he scribbled on his notepad. Mac was responsible for all the project data. He developed most of the specialty software and programming that was used in the development process and for tracking the upcoming trials.

The last member of the team, Dr. Irene Harris, specialized in toxicology. She was tasked with predicting and assessing any adverse effects from the drug. She explained that one of the primary goals when they were developing CX-232, was to create something that would only impact the protein they were targeting and not damage other cells or proteins. Her enthusiasm was much like Chandler's. She was confident that the drug would sail through the required human trials.

When Coop asked her about Mr. Borden, she became more subdued and, like all the others had no explanation as to how he could have been poisoned or any idea who would have done such a thing.

When Coop was finished, he reviewed his notes and hurried to Amanda's office for his meeting with Neil's assistant. She walked him across the vast expanse of white and glass to the other side of the building. Amanda introduced Coop to Melissa and left the pair to talk.

Coop looked around and saw no place to sit except the white leather and chrome chairs across the walkway from Melissa's desk. "Is there somewhere we could talk?"

She looked at the office door bearing Neil's name and gave a slight nod. "Let's just go in here."

Coop took a chair opposite Melissa. "I'm trying to piece together what may have happened to Mr. Borden. I'm curious about his interest in selling the business and what you know about that."

"I don't know much. He found a buyer. One of the big pharma companies was interested. I put together a package of all our financial information, and he met with them several times. I know Chandler didn't like the proposal. Neil just kept saying he would get Chandler to come around and see the advantages. I know it was a ton of money."

"Do you have the contact information for the representatives Neil was meeting?"

She nodded. "I'll get you all that I have. They never met here. Neil always flew up north."

"Had Neil been behaving differently prior to his death?"

Melissa's forehead wrinkled. "Well,…he seemed much more intense. He's always been focused on money, but it had become an obsession." She studied the carpet pattern before adding, "He hadn't been himself. He was secretive and distracted. Not like he was when I first met him."

Melissa made copies of the financial package she had prepared and added the name of the buyer, Peter Rusk, and his contact information. Coop recognized by name the pharmaceutical company and their address in New York City and sighed. The last thing he needed was a trip to that overcrowded zoo of a city.

Chapter 4

After dropping the files and logs at the office for AB, Coop and Gus made it back to Aunt Camille's as she was getting the evening meal on the table. Mrs. Henderson had provided homemade soup to go with their leftover meatloaf turned into sandwiches on thick bread, fresh from the oven.

Coop told Aunt Camille about his busy day and all the perks at Borlund Sciences. "By the time I left, I thought I should have gone into the medical field. It's a great place to work. Chandler treats his employees well."

She let him finish telling her about the offices and his plans to spend tomorrow completing his work there before she cleared her throat. "I hate to ask you this. I know how busy y'all are, but you know my friend, Abigail?"

Coop's eyes were wary as he said, "Yeeess, I remember Miss Abigail."

"Well, I told her I would ask you and see if you could spare some time to help her. She's having a problem with her family and needs a new will."

"I'm up to my eyeballs right now. We can make her an appointment for next week."

"She's in an all fire hurry. She said one of her grandsons is stealing from her and she's beside herself. I really can't imagine him involved in any thievery. She's upset with Franklin, the boy's father, and wants to punish him. She wants to cut him off as well as the grandson. She's not in the best of health. The stress of all this has her tied up in knots. Could you please spare a few minutes to talk to her?"

"Franklin? As in Judge Franklin Monroe?"

"Yes, and before you say it, I know, it sounds crazy. Judge Monroe is a fine man, and I've never heard a peep about his son being a problem."

"Did you already promise her I would see her?"

Aunt Camille flashed her impish grin and cast her eyes downward, concentrating on her bowl of soup.

Coop took a breath. "I don't mind helping your friends, but when I'm busy on a complicated case, I don't have a lot of free time."

"I know, dear. It's just Abigail is such a sweet woman, and she's in utter despair over all this. I think she'll feel better if she just has a few minutes to talk to you. You're always so good at remainin' calm and logical. It's probably a big misunderstandin' with her grandson."

Coop couldn't help but admire his aunt's manipulation skills. "I'll see what we can do for her tomorrow, but I'm not promising anything. This thing with Chandler is serious."

She flashed a victorious grin, and they finished their meal. She fixed him some dessert, which he took to his wing of the house. In between bites of pie he studied his notes from the day. He perused the interview schedule AB had set for him. It included the people from the guest log who had accessed the laboratory for CX-232. He also had an appointment with the security company.

There was too much to do, and he hoped to get through his tour of the kitchen and trace the meal from origin to delivery in the morning. If Chandler wasn't the one to drug Neil, it had to be done somewhere in that food chain.

He selected the audio file that had worked before and set it to play before slipping into bed. The sound was calming, but his mind raced instead of relaxed. He tossed and turned as he ran through his conversations with all the scientific team members. One of those five was probably a murderer. At the moment none of them seemed any likelier a suspect than Chandler.

* * *

In an attempt to shake off his lack of sleep, Coop started the day at the gym. His hopes that an intense treadmill workout would revive him were dashed. After a shower, he donned his "I run on coffee with a splash of sarcasm" t-shirt.

AB came in as Coop was pouring his one real cup of coffee. It was massive and held about three servings, but it was an improvement over his past level of consumption. She shook her head and grinned. "It's amazing how you can find so many different rude t-shirts that sum you up—perfectly."

"It's a gift," he said, taking a long sip of the rich brew he loved. "Ah, I needed that this morning."

"I thought your beach waves were working."

"Not so much last night. I'll keep trying."

"I stand by my assessment. It was more the number of those fancy rum and ginger beer cocktails you drank."

"You could be right. Those were delicious."

She grabbed the folder on her desk, and before she made it to Coop's office, she heard a tap on the front door. She turned and looked outside. "Hey, Miss Abigail. Just a sec." She hollered loud enough for Coop to hear.

He came out of his office and rolled his eyes. "Aunt Camille," he muttered.

He greeted Miss Abigail with a smile and took her hand to help her inside. "I didn't know you were coming by so early," he said, helping her to a chair. She was frail and walked with a cane.

"Oh, I just couldn't wait any longer. Camille said you'd help me with my will and I have to get it done."

Coop swiped a clean tablet from AB's desk and sat down on the couch to face the elderly woman. "So, what's going on?"

"That scoundrel of a grandson is trying to steal from me. I caught Trevor rummaging through my desk drawers. He was looking for the titles to Howard's cars. And Franklin has been using checks from my account." AB returned with a tray and handed Abigail a cup of tea.

"I've known Franklin a long time and can't imagine he or Trevor would steal from you or anyone else. Now you're positive he's up to no good? Have you talked to him about it?"

"I'm done talking, Cooper. I want Franklin and Trevor out of my will. It's not fair to Ronald if Franklin and his family are stealing."

"Let me talk to Franklin and see if we can get to the bottom of this. I'm sure there's a logical explanation. He's a successful man and a pillar of the community. Perhaps it's just a misunderstanding."

Abigail's eyes filled, and fat drops fell onto her cheeks. AB offered her a box of tissues and took her cup. "It's unbelievable to me. I can't understand why he would allow Trevor to steal from me and I don't know why he's writing checks. His father and I raised him better than this. I don't deserve such disrespect."

Coop patted her hand. "We'll get to the bottom of this, Miss Abigail. Don't worry about it. I'll talk to Franklin. Then I'll give you a call, and we'll go from there. It won't take long to change your will if that's the course you want to take."

"Oh, it is. I can't have Franklin and his family stealing from me and then give him the same share as Ronald." Her watery eyes stared out the window. "Just the other day, Franklin didn't do his chores. He was off with one of his friends and forgot. Ronald had to take care of it for me. Franklin is the oldest. He needs to be a better example. That boy needs to grow up."

AB raised her brows and looked at Coop. He continued to hold Abigail's hand. "Ah, he's a good kid. I forget to do stuff sometimes myself." He glanced out the window and saw her car askew, parked with one tire up on the curb. "You know, it looks like you have a low tire. I'm going to have AB run you home, and I'll get your tire aired up and back to you. Is that okay?"

Her hands shook as she used the tissue to blot her eyes. "Oh, my, I had no idea. That would be wonderful. I'll phone Howard and let him know you'll take care of the car."

AB pursed her lips and gave Coop a sad shake of her head. Howard, Abigail's late husband, had died more than ten years ago. "I'll get you home safe and sound." AB stood and helped her up before handing her the wooden cane.

Coop walked Abigail to AB's vivid green VW Beetle. Once they pulled away, he ran inside to call the well-respected district judge. He explained what had transpired with his mother and that he didn't feel safe letting her drive home.

Judge Monroe sighed and said, "She's been having a few forgetful spells. I guess it's worse than we thought. I appreciate you taking the time with her. She asked me to sell a couple of the vehicles she doesn't use any longer. I sent Trevor over to go through the desk to get the titles, and she became agitated. I chalked it up to her angst about getting rid of Daddy's collection of cars. She's held onto them for so long, and they cost a fortune to maintain and keep in good running order. I've taken over paying her bills for her, which is why she's talking about her checking account."

"I think she's confused and probably forgetting she agreed to sell the cars. She seems to bounce between the present and the past. She thought your dad was still alive," said Coop.

Coop heard Judge Monroe let out a heavy breath. "I'll have someone retrieve the car and get it back to her. I appreciate the call, Coop. I'll talk to Ronald. We're going to have to face reality about her condition. She's going to need care."

Coop disconnected and rang Aunt Camille. He explained the situation with Abigail and his conversation with Judge Monroe. His aunt let out a sad moan. "Oh, no. I haven't seen her in person for a few months, just talked to her on the phone. I'll make a point to go out and see her this week. Maybe I can help."

Coop checked the time. He hadn't committed to a specific time for his kitchen tour today, but Miss Abigail had put a wrench in his plan. Gus came through the door of Coop's office with his leash in his mouth. Coop couldn't resist his sad eyes and attached it to his collar. "Okay, just a short walk today, Gus."

Gus loved to walk through the neighborhood, sniffing at bushes and trees, greeting those who walked by, and pretending he'd give chase to squirrels. Coop always chatted with Gus on their walks. "You know AB will be back any minute. You'll have to keep her company today since I'm not sure how long I'll be at Borlund. Too bad they don't have doggie daycare. You'd like that, wouldn't you?" They circled a few blocks, and by the time they made their way back to the office, AB's car had returned.

Gus sprang through the back door and darted to AB's desk. "How'd it go with Miss Abigail?"

"Fine, she was confused when we got there. I had to remind her that her car had a tire problem and would be returned to her. I left her with the housekeeper, who had just arrived."

"Judge Monroe is going to talk to his brother about care for Miss Abigail. Aunt Camille is planning to visit her this week. Sad situation."

"I'll get to work on running in-depth backgrounds on the scientific team. You've got that appointment with the security firm this afternoon at their office and then a couple of phone interviews from the guest logs after that. The others are set up for tomorrow and the next day."

"Sounds good. How about plan on coming to the house tonight for dinner? We can get caught up then."

"I'll call Aunt Camille and let her know you invited me." She laughed as she palmed her mug and went to the kitchen to brew a cup of tea.

* * *

Coop checked in with Amanda and Chandler before being paired up with Bernie, the supervisor of the security team. Bernie gave Coop a tour of their security center with state of the art equipment and cameras. Bernie had a friendly but professional demeanor, greeting employees by name as they passed him in the hallways.

He took Coop through the large cafeteria that resembled an upscale food court more than any cafeteria Coop had visited. Bernie explained they served breakfast and lunch daily and offered a variety of choices each day.

He urged Coop to accompany him to the line of food with servers stationed behind it. "I thought we'd start with breakfast. I waited for you, so I'm starving," he said with a quick smile. Bernie selected biscuits and gravy along with eggs and sausage.

With Miss Abigail's interruption, Coop hadn't had time for anything but coffee. He chose a scramble and some toast, filled his cup with decaf and joined Bernie at a quiet table near a massive stone fireplace that dominated one wall of the room. Coop dug into his meal and said, "This is fantastic."

"Yeah, and you can't beat the price. Neil and Chandler treat the employees like family. It's a great place to work. We're all stunned about Neil's death."

"Do you have any theories on who may have killed him?"

Bernie shook his head as he forked another bite into his mouth. "No ideas, but nobody believes Mr. Hollund had anything to do with it."

Bernie echoed Coop's thoughts. "What about the other scientists on the team?"

"I've never seen anything to lead me to suspect any of them would do such a thing. I don't know them as well as I know Mr. Hollund, but find it hard to imagine one of them killing anyone."

"We'll be running an extensive background on each of them and digging into their financials and phone records. Can you arrange for their email and phone records to be sent to my office?" Coop took a sip from his cup and added, "Those of Neil and Chandler as well."

"Sure thing. I'll handle that. Mr. Hollund told me you had full reign and to get you anything you requested."

They finished breakfast, and Bernie led Coop to the kitchen behind the serving line. There was a central kitchen comprised of several cooking surfaces and prep areas that funneled the food to a selection of themed food court type serving areas where employees could choose their meals.

Coop watched the activity of the kitchen staff members dressed in white shirts and black pants, all wearing what looked like puffy shower caps. A handful of workers had embroidered chef jackets and wore colorful head covers. Bernie explained the chefs and sous chefs were the ones wearing the wraps and all the other food service workers wore the disposable bouffant caps that made them look like an army of surgical nurses.

Coop watched the chefs direct the kitchen staff as they moved around the space, toting and wheeling, slicing and dicing, sautéing and baking. It was like a culinary ballet. Bernie motioned for Coop to follow him to an office next to a vast room that served as a pantry and dry food storage area.

Bernie waved a greeting as he came to the open door. "Hey, Arlo. This is Coop Harrington. He's looking into Mr. Borden's death. Mr. Hollund has asked that we provide whatever he needs." Bernie left Coop in the kitchen and promised to meet him when he was finished.

Coop extended his hand to the large man wearing a white jacket embroidered with the title of Executive Chef, who stood to shake it. "Of course. We've been going over things ourselves. Is it true they think he was poisoned?"

Coop nodded. "Yes, I'm trying to figure out who had access to the food that was served at lunch that day. Bernie is giving me a tour so I can get a feel for the process and how vulnerable the food would be to tampering."

Arlo's face fell. The rotund man shook his head as he sat back down in his chair. "I can't imagine any of the staff here doing such a thing. It just sickens me."

"Did you have any new or temporary staff come on board recently?"

Arlo paused in thought. "No, I double checked everything when the police came through. Nobody new or temporary on staff that day."

Coop continued questioning Arlo and had him walk through the food preparation related to the lunch served to the partners. Arlo explained they had a selection of recipes favored by both men and were notified via email or a call from one of the assistants if the partners would be having lunch in their private dining room. It was left up to Arlo to choose the menu.

Arlo or one of the senior sous chefs would prepare the food, and when it was ready, it would be delivered via the service elevator. The delivery was handled by one of a few top kitchen staff or one who had done great work and was chosen to serve lunch to the partners in recognition of a job well done. The meal always consisted of soup, followed by an entrée and salad, plus dessert.

"I've gone over the meal from that day several times. At first, I thought maybe it was a food allergy or something weird, but it all checked out." Arlo shook his head and handed Coop a piece of paper. "Here's the menu for the day."

Coop studied the items, noting the chicken tortilla soup, followed by soft tacos with a green salad and chocolate lava cake. "Sounds delicious. Do you remember who delivered the meal?"

"Yeah, I don't normally pay much attention to that, but after Mr. Borden, well, I wanted to make sure we hadn't messed up. Jake, one of our junior sous chefs, delivered it. I quizzed him, and he didn't notice anything unusual during the delivery. I know the police interviewed him."

"I'd like to talk to him. Can you spare him for a few minutes?"

Arlo nodded and moved into the central kitchen. He tapped a young man on the back and motioned him away from the line. Arlo introduced Coop and offered him the use of his office.

Jake took a seat and licked his lips, his pale face accentuated by the dark circles under his eyes. He let out a long sigh and said, "I've been making myself nuts trying to figure out how Mr. Borden's food was poisoned."

"I know you've been over this many times with the police and Arlo, but I'd like to hear it all again. I'm working for Mr. Hollund, hoping to find out who killed Mr. Borden."

Jake's head bobbed in quick movements. "I understand. None of us can believe Mr. Hollund would do anything like that. Chef had me make the tacos that day. He said they were perfect and asked if I wanted to serve the meal. Of course, I jumped at the chance. It's sort of a reward to serve the partners. Anyway, I plated the entrees and once the trays were ready took them upstairs."

Coop scribbled notes as Jake talked. "Did you stay for the meal?"

"No, not that day. They asked that I serve everything and then leave. Melissa said they had some things to discuss and wanted to be left alone. I placed the soup and salad on the table and left the entrees and dessert on the cart. They both just had water to drink, so that was simple."

"Who made the soup that day?"

"Zach did it that day. He's a senior sous chef and does most of the soups. It's his signature dish and one of the most popular soups we serve. We even ran out of it at lunch that day."

Coop continued to question Jake asking if he had left the cart with the food unattended at any point during delivery. Jake recounted the steps he had taken to deliver the meal. The only time the food was out of his sight, was in the private dining room. He had been alone in the service elevator. He recalled seeing a few people in the hallway, but the food had been covered the entire time. He never stopped with the cart, except to check in with Mr. Borden's assistant.

"Was she ever alone with the food?" asked Coop.

Lines appeared on Jake's forehead as he contemplated the question. "I don't think so. I'm trying to remember if she came in the room after she opened the door for me."

"Take your time. Close your eyes and picture the day in your mind. Focus on her opening the door for you and then what did you do?"

Jake's eyes closed and Coop remained quiet to let him concentrate. "I'm always flirting with her. Nothing serious, but she's cute, so I try to be clever. I bragged about making lunch and, yeah, she did come in with me. She was there when I got the tablecloth out of the closet and set the table." He opened his eyes. "I guess she was technically alone with the trays while my back was turned."

"Great, that's great, Jake. So, let's keep this conversation confidential. It doesn't mean anything at this point. I'm just trying to check things out and make sure nothing has been missed. I'll follow up with Melissa."

Jake made a zipping motion near his lips. "I understand. I'm freaked out enough by all of this. I won't say a word."

Coop thanked Jake and sought out Arlo to get permission to wander through the area and watch the food preparation. Coop surveyed the action and scanned the ceiling and walls for cameras. He noticed cameras positioned along the serving line and one installed to encompass the food storage areas. He saw only one camera in the general kitchen area.

Coop made a few notes and checked in with Arlo before leaving. "Could you check your records for any staff members who were out the day of the event or the next day?"

Arlo punched keys on his computer and shook his head. "Sorry, nothing the day of. We have two people out the day after. Marco is still gone. He was scheduled for vacation. He's taking his wife on a fancy cruise and won't be back for a few more weeks. Monica was out the day after, again a pre-arranged day for a doctor's appointment."

Coop nodded his thanks and made his way back to meet Bernie. He took him on a ride in the service elevator and showed Coop the path to Mr. Borden's office. The halls were quiet as they made their way to Melissa's desk. Bernie waved a hello and Coop said, "We wanted to take a look at the dining room where the partners had lunch."

Melissa stood and smiled at both men, leading them down a long hallway past a conference room to a locked door. She unlocked the door with a key and held it open for them.

The room was large and was set up with a round table fit for two diners. "I expected a small room," said Coop.

"It serves several purposes. It was designed for private gatherings. Mr. Borden used it for hosting vendors or other guests. Mr. Hollund didn't socialize much and usually only used it when there was a group gathering like a celebration for the team or something like that. He and Mr. Borden ate lunch here a few times a week."

Coop wandered around the room, noting the location of the closet, which was at the far end of the room, away from the table. "Jake tells me he delivered lunch the day of Mr. Borden's death. I understand you were also in the room when he was setting up the luncheon?"

She nodded. "That's right. I like to make sure everything is ready for the two of them."

"Did you notice anything strange that day? Were the covers on the food when Jake arrived?"

"Nothing seemed out of the ordinary. As I recall, the covers were on the food. We chatted while he set up the table. Many times the server stays in the room or close by, but Mr. Borden asked me to have him leave lunch and not stick around. He wanted to talk to Mr. Hollund about selling the business and didn't want to be disturbed."

"Did you handle the food that day?"

Melissa's smile disappeared, replaced with a grimace. "I certainly did not. I don't like your accusation, Mr. Harrington."

Coop held up his hands. "No accusation here, just asking questions. So, did Jake uncover the food before he left?"

"He removed the covers from the soup and salad. He left the entrees covered so they'd stay warm." Her tone was clipped and lacked any warmth.

"Is it possible anyone could have entered the dining room between the time the food was set up and Mr. Hollund and Mr. Borden arrived?"

She shook her head. "I don't think so. After Jake left, I used the phone to let Mr. Borden know lunch was ready and he came in a few minutes later. I left and didn't see anyone else, except Mr. Hollund when he walked by my desk."

"So, Mr. Hollund arrived when Mr. Borden was already in the room?"

"Yes. I suppose Mr. Borden could have left the room before Mr. Hollund's arrival, but I have no way of knowing."

"The only access to the room requires a visitor to pass by your desk, right?"

"Right...well, except for Mr. Borden's private elevator. Each of the partners has his own elevator that serves his office. So, I guess someone could have come up the elevator to his office and then out into the hallway and to the dining room."

Bernie added, "The private elevators require a key card and are only open to the partners and their assistants, plus security, of course."

Coop's eyes squinted as he nodded. "Could I see the elevator, please?"

Bernie ushered him out the door and Coop thanked Melissa for her time. They wandered down the hallway, and Bernie used his key card to open Mr. Borden's office. He directed Coop to an alcove behind a false wall and showed him the elevator. Bernie hit the button, and the doors opened. He showed Coop the card reader and pressed the button for the lobby. The elevator didn't move until he placed his card against the reader.

Coop and Bernie exited and were in another niche on the ground floor hidden from the main hallway across from a set of restrooms.

It was next to another elevator, Mr. Hollund's, which went from the lobby to his office. Bernie motioned to it, "They didn't use these much. It was part of the initial design, but unnecessary. It's not like it's a twenty story building."

Coop nodded in agreement. "Was there any activity in the elevators on the day of the murder?"

"Mr. Borden used the elevator in the morning when he arrived and then again later in the morning. It's in your logs."

"Thanks, I still need to review those details."

Bernie added, "I've gone over the video footage for the day of the murder and haven't found anything suspicious. We don't have a huge number of cameras. They focus primarily on the entrance points. Nothing in the stairwells and nothing in the labs. I argued for cameras in there, but Mr. Hollund insisted none be installed to limit access to research. Corporate espionage and all."

"I can understand his point. I'm just looking for something that would lead us to the real killer. I get the feeling nobody thinks Chandler is capable of murder."

Bernie shook his head. "I would agree. He's not the type."

Chapter 5

Coop thought about Melissa and the fact that she had been alone with the food as he made the drive to Omni Security. After spending an hour talking to their technicians and owner, he was convinced the likelihood of tampering was low. They showed him how the computer-controlled system kept a log of all actions, including administrator activities.

Chandler's office had arranged for Omni to run a complete check and share their findings with Coop. There had been no overrides during the day of the murder. The last bypass of the lab door had been months ago for Dr. Harris, who had left her badge at home.

They also verified the only cardholders with total access were Chandler and Neil, along with the security officers. Coop studied the reports. "Can you tell if there had been access given to the lab door previously and then removed?"

A technician punched a few keys on the keyboard and brought up a screen. "No, no changes to access groups for that door in years. Just those seven people have access. Nobody else has ever been granted temporary access."

Coop took the report, thanked them, and headed back to Harrington and Associates.

* * *

He found AB at her computer with Gus snuggled close to her chair. "I was getting worried that you would be late for your interviews," she said.

Coop rushed to his office, "I know. It took longer than I thought and from what I can see the key card system is solid." He slid into his chair and used the sheets AB had organized to make his first call.

Thirty minutes later he emerged from his office, running his hands through his hair. "That was a bust," he said, plopping onto the couch. "The salesman for the scientific equipment company dropped off new catalogs and brought lunch for the team. He didn't even get close to the room with the vials. He was only in their small conference room."

"What about the guy from the FDA?" she asked.

"He was there to meet with Dr. Swenson to discuss the upcoming human trials. He was interested in the patient room and the protocols. He didn't go into the lab or the room with the CX-232." Coop leaned back and stared at the ceiling. "Neither of them noticed anything out of the ordinary."

"I've got some backgrounds done on a few of the suspects. Still running the rest of them."

"Add Melissa Schwarz, Neil's assistant to that list. I learned she was alone with the soup before the two partners arrived. The only other person, who was alone with it, was Jake Chapman, one of the sous chefs. We'll need to background him."

AB nodded. "Got it. I should have all these done by tomorrow."

"I'm going to take the video footage home tonight and start looking at it. Figure it may work to put me to sleep."

He whistled for Gus, and the dog followed him out the back door and jumped into the Jeep. After a filling meal, he retired to his home office and brought up the camera footage from Borlund Sciences.

Gus settled into his chair. His eyes struggled to stay open as he watched Coop staring at his computer screen. Coop focused on the lab door for his first review. The footage covered the week leading up to Neil's murder. He watched as the scientists he recognized entered and left the lab. Nothing looked out of place. He saw the janitor arrive in the evening and get escorted through the door. He couldn't see the interior of the lab but noticed each janitor spent no more than twenty minutes inside before exiting with a supply cart.

Neil didn't visit each day, just a couple of times the week before his death. He was carrying a folder and didn't spend much time inside the lab. The last time he was there was the day before the murder. The only team member in the lab at the time of his visit was Chandler.

The evening prior to the murder Chandler worked late. He left the lab around eight and returned with his briefcase minutes before ten. He spent less than fifteen minutes inside before exiting. Coop made a note of the times so he could follow up on Chandler's activities when he wasn't working in the lab.

Coop moved to the camera footage that covered the entrance area to Neil's office suite. The camera captured only the hallway outside and the entry, including Melissa's area. Coop's eyes tired as he watched the mundane activities inside the building. On the day of the murder, he didn't see Neil enter the office, which matched with Bernie's account of him using the private elevator.

He saw Neil on camera when he approached Melissa's desk with a folder and then retreated in the direction of his office. Neil left the office suite around ten-thirty and Coop knew from the access records he returned via the elevator at eleven-twenty. He watched Jake come down the hallway with the tray of covered food and saw Melissa lead him away, off camera, to the dining room.

As Jake said, he returned without the meal cart, after seven minutes, which was a reasonable amount of time to set up the table.

Melissa didn't return until a few minutes before Chandler walked into the angle of the camera and crossed in front of her desk on his way to the dining room.

He made a few more notes on his pad before calling it a night and turning off the screen. Melissa, Jake, and Chandler were the most likely suspects unless he could find evidence of someone else tampering with the food from the kitchen to the hallway. He made a mental note to contact Bernie and ask him for help in finding the correct cameras to watch Jake's trip with the service cart.

* * *

Coop started on the footage again the next morning. He found Chandler on camera entering his office after he left the lab the evening before Neil's murder. He saw him leave and return a few minutes later with a dinner plate. Coop watched him depart again before his ten o'clock appearance at the lab. He was toting his briefcase and his coat, as he turned out the lights to his suite. Coop reviewed the footage of Chandler exiting the lab that evening and noticed him wearing a heavy coat and carrying his briefcase. He left the building and didn't return until early the next morning.

Coop checked the time and perused his file on the janitorial staff. They worked the swing shift, so AB had set up late morning appointments with them at the Harrington and Associates office. Only three janitors were assigned to that laboratory. First on the schedule was Tim McCoy.

Tim took AB up on her offer of coffee and settled into a chair at the conference table. Coop went through Tim's employment history and let him get comfortable with the conversation. Then he ran through several questions, and Tim explained the duties in the lab. "One of the doctors followed us wherever we went. We dumped the trash, cleaned the bathrooms, and mopped the floors. Once a week we dusted and vacuumed the conference rooms."

"How often did you visit the drug storage room?" asked Coop.

"Only when we were asked to do the floors. The doctors cleaned all the equipment and counters and kept the whole place spotless. Probably once a week or sometimes every two weeks we did the floor in that room."

Tim went on to explain the area wasn't subject to high traffic, so the cleaning needs of the entire lab were light.

"Were you ever left on your own to do the cleaning without having one of the doctors with you?"

"No, sir. It was a strict requirement for project security. Somebody was always with us."

After a few more questions, Coop thanked Tim and walked him to the front door. The next janitor arrived a few minutes later. AB greeted Charlotte Wyman and introduced her to Coop.

Charlotte was the team leader and a working supervisor. She echoed Tim's account of their work in the laboratory. Coop quizzed her about the security procedures. "We all understand if the drugs aren't approved, business will suffer. We like working at Borlund and enjoy all the benefits we receive. It's a strict policy that we are always accompanied. Many times, Dr. Hollund himself is the one who supervises our work. He works late more than any of the others, so sometimes he's the only one there."

Coop probed more, and she explained the janitors would call into the lab for access or knock on the outer door. "If they're busy, they'll tell us to come back later, so the times we service the area vary, depending on their availability. Some nights all we would do is the bathrooms and a quick trashing. It was by no means dirty, so it never took much time."

She confirmed twenty minutes was a reasonable amount of time to spend in the area. "The only time we'd be in there longer is when we cleaned their breakroom refrigerator or waxed the floors. We always had to prearrange those chores."

The final janitor on the interview schedule was Brett Adams. He was the staff member who serviced the laboratory the night before Neil was murdered. Coop pressed him on his movements that night and Chandler's supervision.

"Dr. Devi was just getting ready to leave when I arrived, so Dr. Hollund escorted me. It was a routine night. Did the regular duties, nothing special."

Coop asked if he and Dr. Hollund chatted while he worked. Brett shook his head. "Not that I remember. Sometimes we'd talk a little, but we all knew not to linger. They had to get back to their work, so we focused on our tasks and left. Mac, uh, Dr. McCutcheon was the friendliest. He liked to talk about sports or stuff going on in town. The rest of them were all business."

Coop continued the interview asking if Brett had noticed anything out of the ordinary or if Dr. Hollund seemed different that evening. Brett frowned. "Nah, I don't think so. He's a pretty serious guy, you know. He worked a lot of late nights, so I always tried to hurry so he could get his work done instead of watching me."

"Was the door to the drug storage room open or closed? Was it locked when you did your work?"

"It was usually closed unless we were doing the floors in there. I couldn't tell you if it was locked since we didn't use it." He thought for a few minutes. "The times I've had to do anything in there, the door was already opened for me. We don't have a key to it. I know that much."

Coop ushered Brett out to the reception area and thanked him for making the time to stop by the office. He clicked the door shut and joined Gus in front of the fire.

"Anything?" asked AB, her brows raised in anticipation.

Coop scrunched his nose. "I don't think so. They were all adamant they were never left alone or unsupervised." He related the conversations and lamented the lack of progress.

He started toward his office and then returned to the couch nearest AB's desk. "Maybe we're asking the wrong questions."

She turned in her chair. "How so?"

"You know how people forget janitors are there. They become almost invisible, like part of the furnishings."

She nodded. "Yep, many times they see and hear things as they blend into the background."

"I was concentrating on their time in the lab and trying to figure out if they had ever been left alone long enough to steal the CX-232. Maybe I need to ask them what they know about the disagreement between Neil and Chandler and the inner workings and relationships at Borlund. The stuff only they see."

"Could shed some light on things. I'd see if you could talk to one of them off the record. Not at Borlund and not here. You could meet for coffee before the start of the janitorial shift."

"Good idea. Call Charlotte and see if we can set something up for tomorrow. She's been there the longest and should know all there is to tell. We could meet her at the dog-friendly bakery. It's close to Borlund." Coop left AB to finish up the backgrounds, and he took Gus with him for a quick stop at Borlund Sciences. He promised Gus he wouldn't be long and sought out Bernie.

Bernie agreed to put together the footage covering the food route and have it ready for him within the hour. Coop's next stop was Chandler's office. Amanda showed him in, and Coop found Chandler hunched over his computer.

"Hey, I just had a couple of questions for you," said Coop, sliding into a chair in front of Chandler's desk.

"Sure, how can I help?"

"Yesterday I discovered Jake from the kitchen delivered your lunch and Melissa was alone with the food while Jake set up the table. What do you know about her? Would she have any reason to harm Neil?"

Chandler's brow furrowed as he contemplated the question. "I don't know much of anything about Melissa. Neil hired her. She's been with us from the beginning. She's polite and does a good job, from what I know."

"Did Neil ever complain about her or talk about her?"

He shook his head. "No, nothing I can recall. He handled all the personnel issues, so I doubt I would have known about it if he did have any issues. I stuck to the science and research."

"Is Melissa close with anyone?"

"Amanda would be a better one to ask. I honestly don't know."

"Okay, and as far as you know Jake wouldn't have a problem with Neil?"

"Again, wouldn't know. He's been in the kitchen for several years. Arlo handles all of them and from what I know does a great job. I've never had any issues with the staff. They do terrific work."

"One more thing. I was watching the camera footage and noticed that Neil visited you in the lab the day before the murder. After everyone else had left. I couldn't see inside but noticed your team leaving one by one before he came in. Do you remember what that was about?"

He sighed. "Yeah, it was another discussion about selling. He wanted to show me how the buyer had increased the offer and how much money we could make. He had a folder with all his figures and wanted to convince me." He removed his glasses and rubbed his forehead. "I told him I didn't have time and that's when he suggested lunch the next day."

"How did you and Neil become partners?"

"He actually approached me. The pharmaceutical arena is its own little world. He knew I was looking to start a company. I had been researching a new drug for diabetic patients and wanted to form a company, confident it would be a success. I was looking for a business partner. He had been working at a small company in California and was leaving and looking for work."

"So you didn't know him before?"

"No. Neil had been in the industry for several years and was well respected. Colleagues of mine knew him and knew of him. He had a good reputation, and when he called, it was an answer to my needs. I couldn't lure anyone with the amount of money we could afford to pay at first but knew the diabetic drug could build the foundation for a great company. I was right. It's made millions for us. We also had great success with a new anticoagulant drug, and now I think CX-232 is going to be our next achievement. It could mean billions."

"So why would Neil not want to wait it out and sell after that when you could get more money?"

Chandler's forehead crinkled. "I don't know. He kept saying it was the right time and CX-232 wasn't guaranteed. He thought we should take the offer while it was there and not bank on something that may not come to fruition. He said we could retire and do anything we wanted."

"The offer was a good one?"

"Yeah, from what I know. It was right at a billion dollars." He shrugged, "As I said, I'm not motivated by money. I had no interest in retiring. I love my work. I tried to appeal to Neil's desire for money to wait on CX-232. He told me he didn't have years to wait it out."

"Why not? What did he mean?"

"I'm not sure. He didn't give me any real answers."

"I watched the camera footage last night and noticed the night before the murder you were alone in the lab for a few hours. You returned to your office and then went back to the lab, wearing your coat, around ten o'clock. Do you remember what you were doing?"

"I've been working late most nights. I was reviewing things for the trial we're starting."

"You went to your office, and it looked like you ate dinner. Then you returned to the lab before leaving the building. What made you go back to the lab?"

"Just to check a calculation. We don't have access to the data outside of the lab. Not even me. It's a security protocol to lock down the confidential research and keep it safe. No laptops to take home. Nothing leaves the lab."

Coop nodded and said, "I'm sure the police are using your visit as more circumstantial evidence. You had unfettered access to the drug when you were alone in the lab. You admitted to being upset about Neil's latest attempt to convince you to sell for a higher offer. It doesn't look good."

Chandler's shoulders slumped. "I know it might look bad, but it's the truth. Check out other nights. You'll see the same activity. I usually go to my office and get caught up on emails and other activities and often return to the lab to work on the project." He paused and said, "I'm tinkering with another idea I have for an immunotherapy drug. My work is almost finished with CX-232. I'll want to see all the results from the trial, but the R&D is done. I'm getting ready to start a new project which means a lot of extra work up here." He tapped his temple.

"Okay, I'll check the footage from other evenings." He gave Chandler his full attention. "I'm not saying you're guilty or they're right. Just trying to take in all the evidence and look for alternative explanations."

"I know. It's just…overwhelming. I still can't believe this is happening."

"Run through the procedures you use for janitors in the lab."

Chandler's description matched what Coop had learned from the janitorial staff. He explained the door to the drug storage room was ordinarily open throughout the day for easy access but closed and locked at the end of the day. The only people who had keys to the room were the team members and security personnel, but they would have to access the lab using the emergency key card.

Chandler reiterated that the janitors were never left alone and also escorted through the area. Coop asked, "Do you think it's possible that your scientific staff could get too comfortable with the janitors and become complacent? Maybe not watch them as closely as you think?"

His lips pressed together as he thought about Coop's question. "I'm sure we're all comfortable with them, but I don't think anyone would slack off on the procedure. The janitors are rarely in the drug storage room, and I know none of the team members would violate that rule."

Chandler's phone buzzed and Coop waved goodbye as he listened to his client slip into a conversation about the human trials. On his way to pick up the footage from Bernie, he stopped by Amanda's desk.

"Hey, Amanda, Chandler thought you'd be the best person to ask about Melissa. What's your take on her? Did she and Neil get along well or were there any problems you were aware of?"

"I'm not aware of any real problems. I know she thought Neil seemed tense these last few months. She said he took a large draw, which he's entitled to do. She just couldn't figure out why he needed the money. She said something about him selling his house, which I know he adored."

"Was that a recent sale?"

She nodded. "I don't know the particulars. Neil didn't tell Melissa. She saw the paperwork on his desk one day."

"Does Melissa have a group of friends at work?"

"Not really. Neither of us does. We get along with everyone and enjoy working with them, but it's easier not to socialize outside of work. We knew when we were hired that our loyalty had to be to the partners and decided early on to keep our work life professional. Neil made it clear he didn't want us befriending employees. That adage about the boss not making friends with his employees applies to his assistants as well. Melissa and I do lunch a few times a month, but even we don't socialize outside of that."

"It seems like everyone gets along well and from what I've been told the turnover is low. People enjoy working here?"

"Oh, yeah, it's terrific. The money is great, and there are a few social events sponsored by the company here at work. The perks are all wonderful. Most people are working long hours. The scientific types are all pretty serious and aren't the most social of animals. It seems to work."

* * *

Upon their arrival back at the office, Coop snagged the folder on Neil and dug into his financials while Gus opted for some ear scratching from AB. "Charlotte agreed to meet us tomorrow at two o'clock," she said, leaving his office with Gus at her heels.

Coop pulled up a map and took a look at Neil's house, which had just sold for two million dollars. The house had sold within a week of it coming on the market. As Coop studied it and other listings in the Franklin neighborhood, he knew Neil should have gotten more for it.

He sifted through the file until he found Neil's address. He studied a copy of a change of address form in his personnel file. Neil had indicated a post office box for a mailing address. Coop recognized the new physical address as that of an apartment. Neil had left a posh area of Franklin for a five hundred square feet studio where he shared walls with students from Vanderbilt.

"So why the sudden downsize?" murmured Coop aloud.

He scanned Neil's financial records noting large transactions once a month. His Nashville bank made regular transfers to a bank in the Caymans. Coop's brows rose as he went further back in the record and saw this had been happening for years. The transfers had started at two thousand dollars a month and then last year increased to five thousand each month. In the last few months, these automatic transfers had been amplified by a considerable amount. They were now up to twenty thousand dollars.

Gus and AB came through the door as Coop finished highlighting the statements. "Get a load of these transfers. We need to see if we can find out what's happening with his account in the Caymans."

"That'll be tough. They don't give up that information. Ben's office may be able to help."

"I've got to talk to him about this anyway. I can't believe his team didn't think this was strange. Where is all this money going? Not to mention the proceeds from the sale of his house. Get in touch with the realtor on it and see what we can find out about it."

"Will do." She set the rest of the files on his desk. "I did a quick scan of the other members of the team. Nothing jumped out. See what you think."

Coop pulled Melissa's folder next. He scanned her information and saw nothing in her financials to indicate a problem. No large deposits or withdrawals. She was paid a good salary and spent every penny. He perused the credit card statements and noticed a few charges to places he spotted as online gambling sites. They hid behind initials, but he recognized them from other investigations he had conducted.

As he continued to check her statements, he saw a few trips to Evansville, Indiana. It was home to a favorite casino where Nashvillians could take a charter, eat for free, and gamble all day. From the looks of her expenditures, the casino owners netted a healthy profit from their investment in a buffet ticket for Melissa.

"Hmm, I wonder if Melissa has gotten herself in a pickle and needed money. But how could she benefit from Neil's death?"

"Maybe she gets something in his will," suggested AB. "The only beneficiary of his life insurance is Chandler."

Coop scribbled a note on his pad dedicated to questions for Ben. "Have you dug into their social media accounts yet?"

AB shook her head. "Next on my list. I'll call the realtor and start looking online for any connections between our suspects and Neil."

Coop continued to look through the folders for each of the team members. He studied Chandler's financials. He made a ton of money, as did Neil, but no weird transactions. He saved most of it and donated a substantial portion to charity. He had a pricey house near Belle Meade and an expensive car, but other than that didn't spend much. From looking at his credit cards, he used them for gas, an occasional restaurant, and books.

Coop picked up the phone. "Hey, Chandler. Sorry to bother you, but I'm going through backgrounds and financials and see that Neil has some sort of account in the Caymans. Do you know anything about it?"

"We both have accounts in the Caymans. Neil and our accountant set them up for us. We deposit the income from our foreign sales into those accounts to avoid a tax burden. I'm not an expert, but our legal guys tell us we can do that with foreign income."

"Do you know why Neil would be transferring money each month into his Cayman account?"

"No, I don't do anything with mine. Just let it accumulate. Someday I guess I'll have to do something with it. I'll let the lawyers and accountants figure it out. I can get you copies of the statements for both accounts. We have them here at the office."

"That would be great. Just fax them over to me." He paused and tapped his pen on his notepad. "Did you know Chandler sold his house in Franklin and moved to an apartment not far from your office?"

"No, he hadn't said a word about it." He sighed and added, "As I said, we didn't have much of a personal relationship outside of work. I do know he loved that house. I remember when he bought it and invited me to a housewarming of sorts. It doesn't make sense that he would sell it and move to an apartment. The company is thriving. Was he having money issues?"

"It looks like he may have been. I'm still digging into it. I'll keep you in the loop."

He hung up and continued to study Neil's folder. He stuck a note on the outside of the file and Gus followed him to AB's desk. He told her to expect a fax from Chandler with the Cayman account information. "I'm beat. See you in the morning." Gus gave AB a quick lick on the hand before hurrying to catch Coop.

Chapter 6

Breakfast Friday morning at Peg's Pancakes morphed into a meeting at Ben's headquarters. Over waffles and eggs, Ben's interest piqued when Coop shared his findings. Ben put in a call to Kate and Jimmy and asked them to meet at the precinct. Coop, with his list of anomalies, was stationed at the conference table while Gus rested on his well-used bed in Ben's office. After running through Coop's discoveries, Ben shook his head. He pointed to the signatures of the detectives on the report. "These two are out on another case at the moment, but they've got some explaining to do about this one." Ben slapped the case file down on the table with a loud crack.

"AB and I spent all day yesterday trying to get information from the bank in the Caymans. It's apparent Neil had more than one account. The only transactions listed on the statements Chandler faxed over were related to foreign sales through Borlund Sciences. The bank wouldn't budge on discussing any other accounts."

"We'll get started on that angle, but it will take time. They're not known for sharing information. That's why so many people hide money down there." Ben shook his head in disgust and waved Kate and Jimmy over to the table.

They listened as Coop outlined what he had learned about Melissa and Jake having had time alone with the food and the apparent financial problems Neil had been experiencing in the months before his murder. "I know Chandler looks like the guy for this one, but it's all circumstantial. There's more going on here than we know."

Kate studied Coop's notes and said, "We've got to get to the bottom of all this money moving around. That could definitely lead to a motive."

Ben agreed. "I can see how the other two honed in on Chandler. He's the only one with a motive and access to the drug, but Neil's financial issues are compelling reasons to dig deeper."

Kate frowned. "Maybe one of the others on the team doesn't seem to have a motive, but was used as a way to get the drug for someone outside of the company?"

Coop bobbed his head. "I've been trying to think how that could have worked. Someone in Neil's world would have had to hire or bribe someone on the team to kill him. I didn't see anything in their backgrounds that would lead me to that conclusion, but I'm willing to till the soil again."

Kate drummed her fingers on the table. "I wouldn't discount Jake or Melissa just yet. Maybe one of them got to a team member." She stared at the wall in thought. "Maybe someone got access to the drug not based on the notion of using it to kill Neil. What if someone said they wanted to use it to try and help a patient? Someone close to them suffering from Alzheimer's."

Coop's eyebrows arched. "That would make more sense. Appealing to a doctor's emotions is more plausible than getting one of them to be an accomplice to murder."

Ben closed the cover on the case file. "Okay, let's concentrate on the accounts in the Caymans and get that request in the pipeline. We need to take another look at all those scientists and see if any of them could have been persuaded to share some of the new drug. Once that's done, Kate and Jimmy can dig into Melissa and Jake and anyone else in the kitchen that could have tampered with the soup. I know we looked at the guy who made the soup and the lab tested the dribble that remained in the pot. No trace of any of the drug."

Coop nodded. "The drug was added to Neil's bowl, either in the kitchen, on the way to the dining room, or in the dining room. Chandler is the only one who had access to the drug and the soup, but I think it's more convoluted than that."

Kate and Jimmy nodded, and Ben said, "I think we need to look into Neil a bit more. We messed up on this one. I'll be talking to the other two detectives, but Kate and Jimmy will be taking the lead on this. Problem is we've got a mess of cases right now, so it's going to be slow."

Coop stood and said, "I'm going to dig into the sale of the company and Neil's obsession with that idea. He was involved in some sort of serious financial trouble, and it looks like he thought that was the solution."

Gus darted from Ben's office and made the rounds for a few nuzzles from the group at the table and scored a couple of dog treats before he followed Coop outside to the Jeep. Back at the office, they found AB at her computer researching Peter Rusk.

Coop poured himself a cup of decaf and made AB a fresh cup of tea. He plopped onto the couch and said, "Did you learn anything interesting?"

"Rusk is a VP at FuturePharma, the third largest pharmaceutical company in the United States. He's been with them for most of his career. His specialty is acquisitions. He's made some great moves that have gained them some of the most prescribed and profitable drugs." She rattled off a few of their popular drugs.

"I recognize their names from all those horrible commercials on television. The ones that have a happy voiceover point out all the terrible side effects, including death, while people walk through flowered meadows and smile."

"That's them. Their revenue was over fifty billion last year."

"Whew, that makes Borlund look like a lemonade stand."

AB nodded and sipped her tea. "And their purchase would have made Chandler and Neil half a billion dollars each."

"I need to talk to Mr. Rusk. I don't want to make a trip to New York, especially in winter. See if he's willing to chat on video with me."

"Got it, I'll set something up for next week."

Madison and Ross were in the office preparing for their shift tonight. They agreed to watch the phone while AB and Gus met with Charlotte. As they neared the bakery, Gus trembled with excitement. He loved the place and the free samples he scored. He bounded from the Jeep and herded Coop and AB to the door.

Charlotte was already waiting at a table in the back of the bakery. Gus made a beeline for his favorite worker and received a pumpkin cookie as a reward. He munched it down, followed by several loud slurps from the bowl of water set aside for the bakery's canine customers.

AB joined Charlotte, and Coop fetched their drinks and plate of assorted cookies. He slid into the chair, Gus at his feet content to nibble on another free sample. "Thanks for meeting us, Charlotte. We're curious about your impressions and knowledge of the relationships at Borlund. Off the record, of course."

"You mean more of the gossip and rumors around the place?" she said with a nervous laugh.

He smiled. "I'm interested in anything that could shed light on a motive for Mr. Borden's murder. Anything out of the ordinary related to Dr. Hollund or anyone on his team working on CX-232."

AB added, "We know from experience with other companies that janitorial staff members often see and hear things during the course of their duties. Sometimes people forget you're there and do and say things that could help in our investigation."

Charlotte pondered as she took a sip of her coffee.

Coop said, "When we talked before we went over what happened in the lab. We're curious about other areas you clean. Private offices of the team members or other areas."

"For the most part, it's a great place to work. People are happy, so there's not a lot of drama." She hesitated and said, "I hate to bring this up. It seems like pure gossip." She took a breath. "I walked in on a compromising situation. With Mr. Borden."

Coop and AB waited for her to explain. "One of the women from accounting was in his office after hours. It happened twice. I walked in on them and left quickly."

"Who is the woman from accounting?" asked Coop.

"Her name is Gina Preston. This was several months ago, so I'm not sure it's still important. She left the company not long after that. I never said anything about what I saw." She shrugged. "Mr. Borden was the boss. His personal life is none of my business."

"Did he threaten you?"

She shook her head. "No, he never said a word about it."

"What do you know about Gina?"

She shrugged. "Not much. I think she's married, judging by the photos in her office. She has kids in college. I didn't really know her."

They chatted for a few more minutes and prodded as much information as Charlotte could recall. She didn't know where Gina went when she left Borlund and had never seen further inappropriate behavior on the part of Mr. Borden.

Charlotte checked her watch and said, "I gotta run and get to work. Thanks for the coffee and please don't say I said anything. I wouldn't want anyone to think I'm a blabbermouth."

Coop and AB assured her they wouldn't divulge her identity. After she left, they lingered over their treats. "What do you think?" asked AB.

"I think she's being truthful. She's loyal. Values her job. Keeps her head down and doesn't want to get involved in office drama."

"That's my impression. I guess we need to find Gina and see what she can tell us." She gathered her things and slipped Gus the last bite of her pastry. Coop bought a bag of their pumpkin dog treats, and they all headed back to the office.

AB hollered out a hello to Madison and Ross and settled in at her desk to research Gina Preston. Coop put in a call to Bernie to see if he could tell him anything about Gina's history at Borlund.

Coop jotted a few notes and thanked Bernie. He wandered out to refill his cup and see what AB had learned. "Bernie suggested I talk with Gina's supervisor. I'm going to give her a call and see if I can meet her in the cafeteria at Borlund."

"Nothing noteworthy in her background. Married, two kids. Both in college. Husband is an assistant sales manager at a car dealership. No credit problems, nothing suspicious. She's working another accounting position at that big firm in Green Hills, Kramer and Dune."

"Could be just a run of the mill affair. I asked Bernie if he knew anything about Neil and Gina." Coop shook his head. "He said he'd never heard anything. Didn't know Gina well. Said she was always polite and did her job. Didn't stand out, one way or the other."

Coop meandered back to his office and dug into the one small package of chocolate covered peanut goodness he allowed himself each Friday. He popped a few into his mouth, intent on making them last all day.

As he pondered the case, AB buzzed his phone. "Hey, Coop, I've got your mother on line one. She's calling collect."

He shook his head and let out a long sigh before picking up the phone. "Cooper Harrington," he said.

"Coop, it's me, your mother. I told your girl it was me, didn't she tell you?"

"Yes, Mom. What do you need?"

"I'm in a bit of trouble. I, uh, I'm in jail."

Coop's fingers tightened on the handset. "Are you still in Vermont?"

"Yes, yes, I'm here. I'm stuck in some little Podunk town outside of Burlington."

"What are the charges?"

"I'm not guilty."

Coop gritted his teeth. "I didn't ask if you were guilty. What did they charge you with?"

"Identity theft, fraud, and assault on a police officer."

"Sounds like you used a stolen credit card and then when you got caught you took a swing at the officer. Don't answer that. You're on a jailhouse phone."

"I need a lawyer and bail money."

"No bail money from me. I'll see what I can do about finding a lawyer for you. You're going to have to tough it out there for now. Let me talk to the officer with you."

"Cooper, I'm your mother. You can't just let me rot in jail."

"You won't rot, and you're staying. Let me talk to the officer."

Coop listened to Marlene whine and snivel. When he didn't respond, she resorted to calling him every name in the book, but he wouldn't budge. He heard a stern voice in the background and then the crash of the handset hitting a solid object.

Moments later Coop was speaking with Sergeant Gilroy of the Winchester Sheriff's Department. He explained Marlene

Harrington had been apprehended using a stolen credit card and producing a fictitious driver's license in the name of the cardholder. The store manager had called the police, and when a deputy arrived and arrested her, she punched him and kicked him.

"Are you going to arrange for bail? I can give you the names of our local bail bondsmen," offered the sergeant.

"No need. She can be your guest until she goes to court. I'll see if I can find an attorney for her." Coop asked for her case number and jotted down the contact information for the sergeant.

He slammed the phone down and scuttled down the hallway to AB's desk. She saw the fury on his face and said, "What's happened?"

"She's in jail in Vermont." He threw his hands in the air. "Unbelievable. She is such a pain in my backside. All she does is cause me grief and cost me money."

"What can I do to help?" she offered.

He handed her a slip of paper with the information. "See if you can find a lawyer to represent her. I told her I'm not bailing her out of jail. She can sit in there and think about it until she goes to court."

AB eyes widened as she read his notes. "Assault on a police officer?"

"Yeah, she's not going to get away with that one. Punched him and kicked him."

"Oh, my, what was she thinking?"

He pressed his lips together and shut his eyes. "She doesn't think. That's her biggest problem. She gets herself in trouble and then expects someone, mainly me, to fix it for her. I'm sick of it. I just spent a fortune on her trip up there. Granted, I wanted her out of my hair, so part of that expense is on me. I wish she would just disappear."

AB remained quiet, letting Coop ramble and vent. She tapped her keyboard in search of any lawyers they might know in Vermont.

She pointed to her screen, "Here's a private detective who belongs to that association we joined years ago. His name is Wayne Pearl. I'll give him a call and see if he can recommend someone."

"Sounds good. Thanks, AB. His name rings a bell. I think we met at a conference I went to a few years ago." He plodded down the hallway back to his office. His shoulders slumped as he muttered to himself.

While AB put in a call to Vermont, Coop texted his brother to warn him not to answer a call from their mother and told him she was in jail. Moments later his cell phone rang, and he and his brother had a long conversation.

When he disconnected the call, AB came through the door. "Wayne was terrific and connected me with a lawyer in Burlington who is willing to make the trip to Winchester. Her name is Darcy Flint. She promised to connect with your mom first thing on Monday. It's already past business hours in Vermont."

Coop nodded his understanding. "That'll work. She can cool her jets over the weekend in lockup."

"She agreed to bill us next week, so we don't need to wire her a retainer or anything." AB slipped a piece of paper to him. "She'll be in contact Monday and said you could call her anytime." She gave him time to read the details of Ms. Flint's services before adding, "I'll have to call Rusk's office Monday. They were already closed by the time I called."

"No problem. Blame that one on my mom. I'm supposed to foot the bill for her legal issues while she impedes our ability to do our work and make money. Geez, I should just let her use a public defender. She'd end up in jail for years and be out of my hair."

"How about we go out and grab a bite to eat tonight? My treat." AB gave him her best cheerful smile.

Coop chuckled. "Don't you have anything better to do on a

Friday night than spend time with your grumpy friend who will probably be terrible company?"

She shrugged. "Not really."

"Sounds like the best thing to distract me. I'll run Gus home and let Aunt Camille know what's going on. Give me an hour?"

* * *

Coop's weekend consisted of a mixture of rest and activities to distract him from his mother's current situation. Aunt Camille invited AB to join them for movies on Saturday. They both steered clear of the topic of Marlene and focused on memories of their holiday trip.

After lounging around for most of the day, Coop took Gus on a long walk Sunday, past Silverwood and all the way to the stairs at Percy Warner Park. Gus loved to run up the stone steps, and it beat the boring treadmill Coop had grown to hate. Getting outside in the crisp air and working up a sweat helped clear his mind of thoughts of his mother and her latest escapade. He even had time to straighten his home office and organize the upcoming week, hoping for no further setbacks.

Sleep was elusive over the weekend, but Coop was able to catch a few naps to make up for it. Even the long walk Sunday afternoon didn't prove to be the magic bullet for his insomnia. In between ideas about Chandler's case and surges of infuriation with his mother, he captured only a few hours of precious sleep.

In the still dark hours of Monday, Coop met AB at the gym. After a shower and breakfast, he and Gus made their way to the office, where AB was already on the phone. He poured himself a cup of decaf and got to work on Neil's folder. He studied his notes and then transferred items of importance to his large whiteboard.

Melissa and Jake dominated two columns, along with a list of financial peculiarities related to Neil. The last column included items he wanted to check pertaining to kitchen staff access to the soup and the theory of Chandler's team members being used to access the drug for someone else. He added Gina's name to the last column.

He knew it would be days, possibly weeks before they had anything definitive from the Cayman Islands. His phone sounded, announcing the realtor who listed Neil's house returning his call.

After several minutes of conversation, he hung up and added a few notes to his board. AB walked in holding a large gift basket wrapped in colorful cellophane and decorated with a glittery ribbon. "This just arrived for us. It's from Judge Monroe and his family. The note says they appreciated our help and that Abigail is going to be moving to a memory care center next month."

"Poor Miss Abigail," he said. "That's thoughtful of them to send us something. Unnecessary since we didn't do much."

She unwrapped it and announced the contents. "It's fun to get something unexpected." She stacked up the loot on the table and said, "We could eat on this for weeks."

Coop saw the bottle of wine amid all the cheese and fruit and snacks. "Take the wine home with you. I'll give Judge Monroe a call and thank him." He shook his head. "Aunt Camille will be heartbroken over Miss Abigail moving."

"I'm sure she'll go see her often. It will give her a new purpose. She likes being needed."

"Well, back to the case," said AB, cradling the wine. "Did you learn anything new from the realtor?"

He shrugged. "Not really. He just confirmed what I had guessed. Neil was in a hurry to get the house sold. The realtor tried to convince him to price it higher, but Neil jumped on the first cash offer, and it sold within a week." Coop leaned against the conference table. "He didn't have any idea why Neil was in a rush. Said the house was almost empty and he wanted to bring in items to stage the house, but Neil refused."

"Hmm…so, the time factor was more of a priority than the amount. Interesting."

"One bright spot, he was able to give me the account number Neil had them wire the money to in the Cayman Islands."

Her eyes danced with excitement. "Well, that's a big lead."

"Yeah, I'll give it to Ben and see if it will help move things along." He added numbers to the financial column on the board. "When the mortgage was paid, it left him with less than a hundred thousand dollars. The realtor insisted Neil could have gotten more if he had been willing to be patient."

"We need to see the activity on that account and find out what's going on and where that money is going," she said, hurrying to Coop's desk to answer the ringing phone.

She placed the call on hold. "It's Darcy Flint."

Coop nodded and picked up the phone. AB made for the door, but Coop motioned her to stay. After thanking the lawyer for her quick response, they had a short conversation. Coop ended it with, "I understand. Thanks again."

AB gave him a quizzical look over the rim of her cup of tea. "Ms. Flint says Mom used a credit card and driver's license that her friend Ruben gave her. He's also in trouble and currently incarcerated. She said she could probably work with the credit card problem, but the assault is another story. She's going to talk to the DA and see if there's any chance of reducing those charges."

"So, she could end up staying in jail?"

"Yep. I think that might be the best place for her. Room and board are provided. It's a small town. County jail, not a prison. Maybe she'll come to her senses in there." He handed AB a note.

"This is what we need to send to Ms. Flint to cover her fees. I'm not risking any bail money. She's way too flighty. There won't be a trial. Either she gets a better deal for her or Mom will have to take the punishment. No question, she assaulted the officer, and I'm not inclined to do anything more to help her get out of it." He rearranged the papers on his desk and muttered, "It's about time she suffers a consequence."

AB nodded and slipped the note into her pad of paper. "Okay, I'll send out a check today." She glanced at her notepad. "I talked to Mr. Rusk's assistant. I explained our situation, and she talked to him and called me back. He had learned of Neil's death when he called Borlund and is eager to help. He can squeeze in a video call tomorrow early in the morning. Like six our time."

Coop let out a long sigh. "That beats a flight to New York. I'll be here." He donned his jacket and said, "I'm going to run over to Borlund and meet with the accounting supervisor and see what I can learn about Gina."

Bernie, true to his word, had arranged a meeting in the cafeteria. Coop slid into a chair across from a woman with short gray hair. Bernie introduced her as Leslie Wells. Coop explained he was investigating the death of Neil Borlund and he had come across a connection with Gina.

"Did Gina have occasion to interact with Mr. Borden on a regular basis?"

Leslie shook her head. "I wouldn't say regularly. She did some work, as all the technicians do from time to time, on a project for him last year. That's the only time I recall her interacting with him. She had a few meetings."

Coop quizzed her about Gina's personal life. "She kept to herself for the most part. I know she had two children in college and was married. She never mentioned much about her private life."

Leslie continued to describe Gina as a hard worker who was quiet and a bit of a loner. She didn't socialize much and ate her lunch at her desk.

Coop asked, "Do you know why she left Borlund?"

"She landed a great job over at Kramer and Dune. Much more prestigious and a bigger salary." Leslie took a sip from her coffee. "I was surprised. She didn't seem to the type to seek out a new position."

Leslie opened Gina's file and shared her contact information and the date she left the company. She'd worked at Borlund for three years. Coop scribbled notes on his pad and noticed she resigned from the company around the same time as the transfers to Neil's Cayman account increased.

"Did you have any reason to suspect Gina was having an affair with Mr. Borden?"

Her forehead creased. "No, I never saw any behavior by either of them that would make me think that. Do you?"

"Oh, no, ma'am. It's just something that came up in the investigation, and we wanted to take a look at it. It could be nothing." He asked her to please keep their conversation confidential and thanked her for meeting with him.

He made his way back to the office and contemplated how to approach Gina. He and AB discussed the options and settled on catching her leaving her workplace for lunch. Calling ahead would give her a chance to come up with a plausible story. Going to her house could jeopardize her marriage. Showing up at work could do the same with her job. They didn't want to cause her any difficulties but wanted to observe her body language and facial expressions when they asked her about Neil.

They made a plan to stake out the parking lot at Kramer and Dune tomorrow starting at eleven. With the threat of Chandler's imminent arrest diminished and Ben redoubling his efforts to explain Neil's financial irregularities, Coop focused his attention on a few other cases for the remainder of the afternoon and got in touch with Judge Monroe.

After ending his call, he donned his jacket and gestured to Gus. He stopped at AB's desk. "Judge Monroe said his mom is going to that upscale facility in Green Hills. It's less than ten minutes from Aunt Camille's house."

"How did Judge Monroe seem?" she asked.

Coop sighed. "Relieved and resigned. He said they'd been getting by with help in the house, but her visit here made him realize how dangerous it was to leave her unattended. That morning the housekeeper came in later, so Abigail was on her own." Coop told her he and Gus were going to cut out a few minutes early to get in a walk at the park before it got too dark.

Invigorated by the brisk air promising to deliver a storm, Gus trotted through the grounds, intent on investigating any smells that piqued his interest. Coop followed along, lost in thought with his hands in his pockets to keep warm. As he huddled his chin further into his coat, the case swirled in his mind like the leaves across the steps.

Chapter 7

Coop, exhausted and bleary-eyed, got to the office before six the next morning and made sure his computer was ready. The late afternoon walk had done nothing to improve his ability to sleep last night. He started a pot of real coffee brewing and built a fire, while Gus supervised from his chair in the office. As soon as the machine beeped, he poured the dark elixir into his oversized cup and made his way to his desk. He took a long swallow, letting the steam transport the cherished aroma.

The wind rattled the windows and the first volley of rain pelted against the glass. After a few more sips, his head cleared and he focused on the screen and his notepad. At straight up six, he heard the telltale sound of a video call and clicked the mouse. Mr. Rusk appeared before him, looking like he'd been up for hours, his dark hair shiny and in perfect order.

Coop was glad he had slipped a jacket over his t-shirt of the day, stenciled with "Those who laugh last think slowest," and thanked Mr. Rusk for making the time for him. He ticked off the questions he had composed and scribbled Mr. Rusk's answers as he listened to the executive.

The interview lasted over thirty minutes, and Coop couldn't think of any more questions. As the conversation wound down, Mr. Rusk offered his direct line and cell number should Coop need more information. Coop disconnected and savored the last few swallows of his coffee.

Gus bolted from the chair, which meant AB had arrived. A few minutes later he heard the door open and the click of the dog's nails as he followed AB to her desk. Coop sauntered out of his office and built a fire in the reception area.

AB sat on the hearth as the flames flickered through the dry logs. "It's miserable outside." She rubbed her hands in front of the orange glow and said, "Did you get any new information from Mr. Rusk?"

Coop nodded and took a seat. "We need to look into another guy, Paul Muller. He's with a pharmaceutical company in California. He's the one who told Rusk about Neil wanting to sell."

"Did Rusk know why he wanted to sell?"

Coop shook his head. "No, nothing concrete. He knew Neil was having trouble convincing Chandler to sell. Rusk kept upping the price, assuming Neil was using Chandler as a negotiating tool."

"I'll dig into Rusk and Muller and see what we can learn about them on a personal level," offered AB.

Coop nodded and glanced at his watch. "It's way too early for California. We'll have to wait a few hours and call this guy and see what he can tell us."

"Did Rusk know Chandler?"

"Nope. He knew of him, by reputation. Says Chandler is one of the most well-respected researchers in the business. He told Neil FuturePharma would keep Chandler on and let him continue to run the research arm. That was one of their last conversations in Rusk's attempt to secure a deal."

"So they thought this new drug would be a huge success? Is that why they wanted to buy Borlund?"

He nodded and stoked the fire. "Rusk says they were sold on the proposal and Chandler's research. Borlund's other drugs are in the top tier of the most prescribed drugs in their segments. He thinks CX-232 is a sure bet."

"And Chandler's whole world and identity are wrapped up in that company."

"Yep. It's his life, and I think he likes to steer his own ship. He didn't want to work for big pharma. He's happy with his modest company and immersed in what he loves. From all accounts, he is respected and liked at work. I didn't hear even the inkling of a bad word about him there."

AB stood and said, "I've got a few files for you to review and some things to sign. Madison and Ross are working the divorce cases and finishing up a few interviews on backgrounds. We can get through those this morning and then it will be time for our lunch ambush.

The weather worsened as the morning disappeared. Coop made a quick trip back to Aunt Camille's to drop off Gus and borrowed her sedan. He and AB planned to invite Gina to join them for lunch, and neither Coop's Jeep nor AB's VW was conducive to another passenger.

They waited in the blustery parking lot, taking care to park near Gina's car. They scrutinized each woman who passed by and were rewarded for their efforts in less than thirty minutes. They both exited Camille's sedan and approached Gina.

AB spoke first and explained they were private investigators working for Borlund and investigating Neil's death. Gina's eyes darted from AB to Coop and then around the parking lot. When she rested her gaze on them, Coop caught a sense of sadness. "We're happy to take you to lunch. We just have a few questions and didn't want to disturb you at work or home," said AB.

Gina was a quick study. "I appreciate that." Coop held the passenger door open, and she climbed into the seat.

Coop drove a couple of blocks to a sandwich place, and they slipped into a booth near the back of the shop. While they waited for their order, Coop began his questions. "During our investigation, we discovered some information that led us to a connection between you and Neil. Could you tell us about your relationship?"

Gina's eyes focused on her lap. "We had a short intimate relationship. I'm not proud of it. It was reckless."

"How did it end?"

"Mutually. I'm not sure how it even started. I love my husband. It was stupid and careless of me to get involved with Neil. I was feeling guilty, and he was, well, distant. It only lasted a few months. A fling, I guess you'd call it."

"Is he why you left the company?" asked AB.

She shrugged. "In a way, but not in the way you think. He told me about the job here. They did some outside auditing for Borlund, and he put in a good word for me." Her eyes brightened. "It's a great job and more money which helps out at home."

They listened as she explained her husband often traveled for his job, and her last child went off to college. She had been lonely, and when Neil paid her attention, it got out of hand. They usually met at his house and never went anywhere in public.

"How about at the office? Did anyone know you were seeing each other?" asked Coop.

"I remember twice we had someone from the janitorial staff walk in on us when we were in Neil's office after work. Another stupid move on our part." She dabbed at her eyes. "That was sort of when I knew I had to stop. I told Neil I thought it best if we end it and he agreed. In fact, he seemed relieved."

A few weeks later he told her about the job, and within a week she had secured an interview. Days later she received an offer. Gina had read about Neil's death in the paper and then saw a follow-up article reporting his death had been ruled a homicide. "I felt terrible. It wasn't like we were soulmates or anything, but I felt horrible that he was dead. Then to find out he was murdered. It was unbelievable."

"You said Neil had become distant at the end of your relationship. Did you notice any other odd behaviors or his part?"

"He was very concerned about what he termed a business deal. Stressed about money." She shook her head. "It didn't make sense because I knew the business was prospering. Nothing had changed in his salary package." She took a sip of her mocha and stared into her cup. "I did enough research for him to realize he was trying to put together a package to find a buyer for the company. Again, with the promise of CX-232, I couldn't fathom the idea of selling."

She had no information about who could have killed Neil. She couldn't think of anyone who harbored a grudge. "We didn't discuss personal issues much. It wasn't that kind of a relationship."

Coop asked, "Do you think Chandler killed Neil? Did you ever see anything between the two of them that would lead you to suspect Chandler?"

She shook her head back and forth. "Never. Neil never spoke about Chandler in a derogatory manner. I never saw anything to indicate Dr. Hollund was upset with Neil. Dr. Hollund had a reputation for being a bit of a nerd. Very focused on the work and brilliant."

They reviewed the dates with her and confirmed his worries had begun around the same time as the increase in the transfers he made to his account in the Cayman Islands. She left Borlund that same month. Gina hadn't talked to or seen Neil since she took the job with Kramer and Dune. The two never emailed or texted.

"I honestly don't know what I was expecting. The best I can figure out, I was lonely, and without something to do, I was enticed by the attention. His house was beautiful. It was like an escape from my life. I never had the delusion that we would be together or anything like that. I wasn't thinking long-term." She sighed. "I wasn't really thinking at all."

Gina answered all their questions, confirming she had never been inside the lab and had never returned to Borlund after she took her new position. She volunteered her contact information and urged them to check her phone. She hadn't talked to Neil since she left Borlund.

They finished their lunch and drove Gina back to her office. She got out of the car and held the door for a few seconds. "Thanks for not coming to my house." She glanced at the building. "Or inside. I'm ashamed of what I did. I know I'll never do it again. I'm sorry for Neil. He didn't deserve to die. I hope you figure it out."

Coop and AB made their way to Camille's to trade vehicles and retrieved Gus. Content to stay indoors after their foray outside for lunch, they warmed themselves on the hearth. "I'll dig into her phone records, but I don't think she's going to give us anything," said AB.

"I agree. She didn't seem to have much knowledge of Neil's activities. She was contrite and sincere. I think it was a mistake she wants to forget."

AB checked the time and said, "I'll make that call to California and see if Mr. Muller will do a video call. I know how important it is for you to observe the interviewee and not just talk on the phone."

As rain lashed against the windows, Coop whittled through a stack of files and business housekeeping chores before studying his notes from his call with Mr. Rusk. Coop meandered to the kitchen in search of a cookie. Gus followed Coop's path, hoping for a morsel. Coop gave him a bite and let Gus out the back door. The dog dashed to a tree and back inside, but was soaking wet from the torrential rain that was beginning to morph into ice.

Coop grabbed a towel and Gus complied with the rub down. He lifted his paws so Coop could dry them. Coop did his best to contain the droplets that flew off Gus as he shook several times. "Okay, big guy, you're semi-dry." Gus hightailed it through the house and planted himself in front of the fireplace in Coop's office.

When Coop walked through, AB was hanging up the phone. "He can make something work later this afternoon." She handed him a slip of paper. "I tried to get it earlier, but seven our time is the best he can do."

"That's fine. It's too nasty to do much of anything else." He continued to his office, eyed Gus, and said, "We won't get our late afternoon walk in this mess." Gus sighed as his eyes fluttered shut.

Coop loaded the video footage from Borlund. His extension buzzed. Darcy Flint was on the line. Coop took a deep breath and hit the button to connect the call.

His hand clenched as he listened to the lawyer. He tapped his pen on a notepad. As the conversation continued, the speed and force of the striking increased. Gus lifted his head from the arm of the chair, concern filled his eyes and his ears perked. Coop uttered his understanding and thanked Ms. Flint before slamming the phone into the cradle. "Unbelievable." He threw the pen on his desk and stomped down the hallway, Gus trotting to keep up with his master.

"You're not going to believe the latest." He slumped onto the couch and Gus rested his head on his thigh.

AB turned from her computer. "Uh, oh. That doesn't sound good."

"They went to court today. Darcy had a lesser charge worked out with the DA for the credit card issue and convinced my mother to accept a deal on the assault charge. It would mean about three more weeks in jail. With Mom's lack of remorse or apology, she said that's the best she could get."

AB nodded her head and swallowed a sip of her tea. "Sounds reasonable."

Coop's brows arched over his widened eyes. "Exactly. They get to court, and good old Marlene has an outburst and tells the judge he's a part of a Podunk scheme like the cops who arrested her. The judge warns her, but in typical Marlene fashion, she doesn't heed the warning. So now she's in jail for contempt. Three days. She'll have to go back and appear again on the other charges."

AB shook her head. "Wow, I would think at her age she would have calmed down a little. It's never wise to antagonize a judge. You'd think the threat of more time in jail would deter her."

"Maturity is not one of her hallmarks." He scribbled on AB's notepad. "Get a check out to Darcy to cover another appearance." He shook his head and added, "Oh, and this is all my fault, according to my mother."

"Coop, you know it's just her being over the top."

"She told Darcy I never do anything for her. I'm embarrassed by her and don't care about her. She can't believe her lawyer-son would let her rot in jail like a common criminal."

"She has a history of not taking responsibility, so it's another way for her to blame someone else," said AB.

"Yeah, it just gets old." He turned his attention to the flames in the fireplace and rubbed his dog's head. "She's right about her being an embarrassment to me. Honestly, if I don't have to think about her or deal with her, it's a good day for me. I care about her, but not as a son. More like as another human being. I don't want to see anything bad happen to her, but I don't want her involved in my life." He sighed. "I know that sounds harsh, but it's the truth."

AB watched but remained silent as he pulled himself off the couch with a groan. "I better let my brother know the latest."

He texted Jack, and within minutes his brother called him. Coop explained their mother's latest escapade. Jack offered to send money to help, but Coop refused. Jack had a family to support and a good job, but Coop knew he didn't have much excess to throw away on something like legal fees.

After the brothers agreed their mother's behavior was beyond foolish, and the chances of her changing were slim, they talked about lighter topics. As when they had chatted before Christmas, Coop promised to make a trip out to Nevada for a visit in the coming months. Coop disconnected and smiled. Talking to Jack always made him feel better. They shared a fierce bond. He never wanted to lose it.

Coop perused his calendar, reasoning when the kids were out of school for a break would be the best time to visit. He stuck a note on his March schedule to check dates and then returned to the case at hand.

He wanted to get a look at the kitchen coverage before he probed further into the staff and their access to Neil's soup. He watched the mundane activities as people moved in and out of camera range, going about the business of meal preparations. He noted the arrival of the first staff members at five in the morning.

The constant movement of all the people dressed in identical outfits made the job of pinpointing any action related to the soup impossible. The camera gave an overall view of the space, nothing up close and personal. He increased the playback speed in an attempt to get through the entire morning before his appointment with Mr. Muller.

There were several large stock pots on the stoves. It was impossible to know which held the soup in question. He hadn't seen anything resembling a suspicious act. He knew the entire batch of soup wouldn't be the problem, but kept his eye on it, hoping to spot when the bowls were filled for the two partners. He studied and squinted at the screen. As the lunch hour approached, the activity level in the kitchen increased. A flurry of white puffy hats filled the screen. Plates and bowls appeared and disappeared. He slowed the whole process down and watched in real time.

AB made sure Gus got a break before she hollered out a farewell and left for the day, locking Gus and Coop inside.

He couldn't make out when or which staff member filled the bowls but saw gloved hands place them on the serving cart stationed away from the prep area. Workers walked between the cart and the camera dozens of times. He saw a couple of bouffant hats leaning over the food and then the view became obstructed with people. The next clear shot showed plates on the tray, and then more activity and the plates were covered.

There was no way to identify anyone from the footage. He'd have to see if Ben's technicians could do anything to enhance the video. He closed the window and pulled out the notepad he had used from his early morning video call.

The call from California came through on time, and Paul Muller filled him in on his knowledge of Borlund Sciences. Muller had the typical look of a beach-loving guy. Tanned, blonde, and relaxed. Coop learned Muller served as the Chief Financial Officer of a mid-sized pharmaceutical firm in Los Angeles. Muller heard Neil was looking for a buyer from a colleague in the San Francisco Bay Area, Derrick Hudson. Muller's corporation had just acquired a number of smaller companies in the last few months. He had his hands full and passed the information to Rusk.

Coop asked him the litany of questions he had prepared for Mr. Rusk, in addition to several others. Muller confirmed Chandler's sterling reputation in the scientific community. He admitted if he had known about Borlund six months ago, it would have bumped one of the other companies he had acquired off the list. Chandler was a hot commodity and was guaranteed to bring in millions if not billions.

Coop ended the call by asking for Hudson's contact information. Muller complied and wished Coop a pleasant evening, sharing he was on his way to surf at the beach. Coop loaded Gus in the Jeep and turned on the defroster while he scraped away at the ice gathered on his windshield. He slid into the driver's seat, rubbing his red hands together, longing for the days he had spent on the warm sand in the Bahamas a few weeks ago.

* * *

The next morning while Coop sat on the hearth giving Gus an extended ear massage, AB put in a call to Derrick Hudson's office. She used the direct line Muller had provided. It rang a few times before a woman answered. She informed AB her boss, Mr. Hudson, was in a meeting all morning. She promised to set up a time he could participate in a video call with Coop. AB stressed the importance and asked that she call back before the end of the day.

Coop gave Gus one last nuzzle and brushed the dog hair from his shirt, which read "When I die, the dog gets everything" and stood. "In addition to finding out more about the potential buyer, Mr. Rusk, let's add Derrick Hudson to our list and see what we can learn about him."

AB nodded and tapped on her keyboard while Coop went back to viewing the camera footage from the kitchen. He concentrated on the staff close to the serving cart and saw nothing definitive. Everyone wore gloves and trying to identify anyone was pointless. The best he could do was estimate the height of the workers. The sous chefs were easy to spot, since they wore the colorful head wraps, but as far as the others went, it was hopeless.

After he exhausted the limits of his software, he sent Ben a text to see if he could get his technicians to enhance the footage. AB came through the door and slipped a sandwich in front of him. "I've got the preliminary information on the three guys." She took a seat and rattled off what she had discovered about each of them while Coop ate his late lunch.

All were wealthy, had families, and had been in the industry for most of their careers. Nothing drew attention in their credit or financial reports. They make a ton of money and spend a ton of money. Healthy bank accounts and credit limits, no bad debts or blemishes on their credit records.

"Looking at their education and employment history, Derrick Hudson and Neil worked at the same small company in California years ago, right out of school." She slid her report in front of Coop. "No longer in business. Neil left there and then partnered with Chandler. Derrick stayed until it was acquired by another company and then he moved on to where he is now."

She flipped a page in her notepad. "I checked out Gina's phone records. She was telling the truth. No calls or texts to Neil. Nothing noteworthy."

Coop nodded as he finished his sandwich and their conversation was interrupted by the ringing of the phone. AB answered, and Coop listened as she set up a time for him to interview Mr. Hudson. She hung up and said, "Five our time tonight."

"Well, that's earlier than I expected." He studied the report and scribbled a few notes while AB dealt with another phone call.

She finished her call and turned her attention back to her notes. "I've also been delving into the scientists on Chandler's team. Their financials look mundane. No recent large deposits for any of them. No recent big-ticket purchases. I need to do more work on their history, but at first glance, it doesn't appear any of them were paid to obtain the drug."

Coop leaned back in his chair. "Chandler's team has to be the connection. We need to find whatever the thread is that links one of them to this and tug at it."

She nodded and said, "I'll keep on them."

He glanced at the whiteboard. "I need to see if Ben has a copy of Neil's will so we can see if anyone else benefits from his death."

"Right. On that front, I did notice a pattern of withdrawals and deposits between Neil and his assistant. Remember Melissa's gambling charges? It looks like a few days before her credit card comes due, Neil makes a cash withdrawal, and she makes a deposit close to the same amount. It's been happening for the last year or so."

Coop's eyes twinkled. "That will give me something to discuss with her. He's probably bailing her out, and she's skimming a little to keep a stash to feed her habit."

"I'll keep looking for more on her."

Coop nodded in agreement. "I'll talk to Ben Friday at breakfast and see what he's learned. Since he hasn't called, he probably doesn't have much."

They continued their research until five when the video call came through. Coop took in the image of the man on his computer screen. Derrick Hudson was unremarkable. A typical guy in a suit and tie. Nothing noteworthy in his appearance. Coop asked many of the same questions he had asked Rusk and Muller.

Derrick had been shocked to learn of Neil's death and told Coop he was happy to help, surprised to learn they suspected murder. Derrick confirmed his ties to Neil through school and then work in California. He hadn't seen him for years but kept in touch through sporadic email or phone calls. Derrick had no clue why Borlund was selling. "Neil let me know about the sale. Said he was looking for a buyer and asked me to steer anybody interested his way." Muller was one of the colleagues he told about the sale.

Coop asked him if Neil had mentioned his partner not wanting to sell, but Derrick said he didn't know anything about it. He, like the other two, lauded praise upon Chandler and commented about his distinguished reputation in the industry. He said his company wasn't in a position to acquire Borlund, but he told several of his contacts.

Coop pressed him on Neil's personal life, but Derrick didn't have a close relationship with Neil. "I think the last time I saw him in person was at a conference several years ago. Our relationship revolved around business more than personal."

After exhausting his questions, Coop thanked Derrick and took down his personal contact information before disconnecting the call. He looked up and saw AB waiting at the door.

"Nothing?" she asked.

He shook his head. "I think it's time to call it a day." Gus trotted behind and bounded into the Jeep. "I'm missing something, buddy," said Coop, as he drove through the wet and windy evening.

Chapter 8

The smell of bacon and coffee greeted Coop when he walked through the door of Peg's Friday morning. Ben was already in their booth, a cup of the warm brew in front of him.

Myrtle appeared as Coop slid across the vinyl seat and poured a stream of Coop's favorite vice into his cup. "We've got a pancake special today if y'all are interested."

They took her up on her suggestion. Coop stirred a healthy dash of sugar into his cup and said, "Anything from the Caymans yet?"

Ben shook his head and smirked. "You're joking, right? They'll drag their feet for weeks. I've got the techs working on the video footage from the kitchen. Kate and Jimmy did a thorough search of Neil's apartment and his car. It was still in the parking lot. They found a burner phone stuffed in the glove box under a bunch of stuff. We're running it down now."

"Hmm. Neil's got a secret. A burner phone, a second Cayman account, a need for money. Something stinks."

Ben nodded. "I can agree there could be another motive related to whatever's going on in his personal and financial life. But Chandler is the only suspect with access to the drug."

Coop's nose wrinkled. "I know. AB is still digging into the team members. Nothing suspicious in their financials. No evidence of one of them getting paid off."

As they focused on their breakfast platters, Coop recapped his conversations with the three pharmaceutical executives. Ben agreed with Coop's conclusion of it being a non-starter.

Ben slid a folded paper from his jacket pocket. "Here's a copy of Neil's will. Nothing odd. His parents and one sister are the beneficiaries. Parents are in California. Sister is in Arizona. They aren't suspects at this point. We did a quick check, and the sister was at work the day of the murder. Parents were home. No record of travel. No credit card charges to indicate they were here."

"Then the money motive for Melissa to kill Neil isn't there. I'm still going to take another stab at her today," said Coop.

"Kate and Jimmy took apart the life of the sous chef who delivered the meal. Came up with zilch."

"I'm not surprised. He seems like a what-you-see-is-what-you-get kind of a guy."

"Unraveling this mess is going to depend on what we can get on Neil's secret Cayman account."

"Not to mention figuring out which one of those scientists took the CX-232 from the lab." Coop took another sip of coffee.

Ben put up a hand in a gesture of surrender. "I know you don't want to hear this, but Chandler is the best suspect."

Coop dipped his head in agreement. "I know, but I don't think he's our guy. There's something else we don't see yet."

"I agree. There's more to this. Swing by later this afternoon and see what the techs found on your footage. Anything else going on with you?"

"Just my mom's court appearance. She's due back later this morning after a relaxing three-day stint in jail. Wanna make a bet her attitude hasn't improved?"

Ben gave Coop a weak smile. "I'm sorry, man. I know she drives you crazy."

"The understatement of the century." Coop plopped some money on top of the ticket and slid AB's takeout container across the table. "I'll see you this afternoon."

The cold damp air made Coop hurry to the Jeep. Gus sat at attention, and his nose moved skyward, sniffing the box Coop carried. "AB will share with you. She always does."

There wasn't enough time for the heater to get warm on their short drive to the office. AB was at her computer when the two arrived. Coop spent the morning staring at his notes and whiteboard, glancing at his watch every few minutes.

At twelve-fifteen, Darcy Flint called. Coop listened to her summarize the hearing and jotted notes as she talked. After he hung up, he grabbed his cup and made his way to the kitchen for a refill and then plopped on the couch in reception and waited for AB to conclude her call.

"Well?" she asked, brows arched in anticipation.

"She got thirty days in jail, community service, and she has to write a letter of apology to the deputy she assaulted. Darcy said Mom at least waited until after she left the courtroom to raise holy hell. Told Darcy she was a moron and should have gotten her off. It was the worst deal she'd ever heard of and stuff like that."

AB shook her head. "Marlene is…well, she's…beyond words."

"I'm looking at the bright side. She'll be out of my hair for the next month."

"Maybe she'll use her time in jail to think about things." Coop grimaced and shook his head. "Well, you never know," said AB.

Coop sent his brother a text to let him know the outcome and asked him to call later when he got off work. He gathered up his notepad and motioned for Gus to follow him.

"I'm going to swing by Borlund and talk to Melissa on my way to see Ben. If I'm not back by five, just close up the place. I'll take Gus with me."

* * *

Coop left Gus napping in the Jeep and found Melissa at her desk. "Mr. Harrington, what brings you by?"

"I had a few follow up questions for you." He gestured to Neil's office. "Privacy would probably be best."

She rose and led the way through Neil's door and took a seat at the conference table.

"We've been digging into financial records and backgrounds on everyone close to Neil. How long has he been loaning you money?"

Her eyes widened, and she ran a finger over her manicured nails. "It's not what you think. We weren't involved romantically or anything."

Coop nodded. "I think you have a gambling problem and Neil bailed you out."

She let out a long sigh. "I guess it is what you think then. I got myself in a little trouble and asked Neil if I could borrow some money."

"And then you got in more trouble and had to keep borrowing instead of paying him back?"

Her eyes wouldn't meet his. "I haven't been back. I'm not going back."

"Melissa, did you have anything to do with Neil's death?"

Her mouth opened and she glared at Coop. "No, of course not. I would never do anything to harm him. I owed him a few thousand dollars, but it wasn't like it impacted him. I was working on saving up and not gambling anymore so I could pay him back."

"Was he pressuring you to come up with the money?"

"No. I was embarrassed about it, but he never said anything. After Christmas, I told him I was done throwing my money away and was going to buckle down and get him paid back. He told me that was fine. He was absorbed in this deal to sell and didn't seem that interested in the small amount I owed him."

"How much did you owe him when he died?"

Her eyes filled and she whispered, "A little under five thousand."

"You should get in touch with Neil's family and let them know."

She nodded and continued to stroke her nails. "I'll do that."

"Other than Mr. Rusk, did you take any calls inquiring about the sale of the company?"

Her forehead wrinkled. "No, not that I remember."

"Does Derrick Hudson ring a bell?" She shook her head.

"He's from California and worked with Neil before."

"I can check the system and see if I have his contact information." She stood, and Coop followed her back to her desk. She clicked her fingers across the keyboard and shook her head. "Nope, nothing on him."

"Can you check Neil's personal contacts?"

Melissa nodded and said, "Sure. Just a sec." More clicking. "Nothing."

"Okay, thanks for your help."

"Do you think Chandler will fire me for the gambling?"

"I don't think so. You haven't done anything illegal."

She nodded her head in quick succession. "I need my job."

"It's wise to get in front of bad news. Better if you control the message and Chandler hears it from you instead of others."

She let out a breath. "You're right. I'll talk to him today." She extended her hand. "Thanks, Mr. Harrington. Sorry, I didn't tell you about it before. When you pointed out I was alone with the soup that day, it spooked me. Then I got scared and felt guilty about the money I owed him."

"One more piece of advice. Find a new hobby, Melissa." Coop dipped his head at her and proceeded to the elevator.

* * *

Coop and Gus made their way to Ben's office, where Gus slurped from his bowl and then snuggled into his bed in the corner. Ben was on the phone and Coop helped himself to a bottle of sweet tea from Ben's mini fridge and slid one across the desk for his friend.

Ben disconnected his call and took a long draw from his tea. "The techs are sending me some enhanced footage. They tried to enlarge the area around the cart and sharpen it a bit. They said it's not great, but better."

Coop told him about his encounter with Melissa. "When I confronted her she didn't deny the gambling or the loans. I don't think she drugged Neil."

Ben's computer pinged. "Here's the footage. I'll put it up on the larger screen." Ben pointed outside his office to a large flat screen mounted on the wall by the murder boards his team used.

Coop and Ben leaned against a conference table and watched as the image filled the screen. The techs had focused on the serving cart, and they watched the action of the staff donned in their white hair caps as they moved across the area. They observed the screen until they saw Jake, wearing a green head cover, wheel it away.

Ben looked at Coop with raised brows. "Again?"

Coop nodded. They started from the beginning and examined it again. With so much activity, it was difficult to focus on the tray. Coop strained and stared at the serving cart, hoping to see something to indicate tampering.

Ben's cell phone rang. "Be right there," he said before replacing his phone in the holder on his belt. "I gotta run. Ask one of the clerks to make you a copy of this. You can take it with you and study it."

He rushed out with a wave and Coop turned off the monitor and poked his head into the office of one of the clerks he knew best. She copied the footage onto a thumb drive. Coop motioned to Gus, and they rode back to Harrington and Associates.

AB met them at the door with a huge smile. "I found something." She followed Coop into his office. "Dr. Irene Harris."

"Okaaaay, what about her?"

"Her sister-in-law's mother has Alzheimer's."

"So maybe she took the drug for her?"

"And maybe Neil found out and threatened her," said AB.

"Might as well shake that tree and see what falls out." He glanced at the clock. "It's almost five on a Friday. I'll head over to Borlund first thing Monday morning. Let's call it a day."

Coop shut off his computer and pocketed the thumb drive. He waited for AB to finish at her desk and they walked out together. "Aunt Camille wanted me to invite you to Sunday supper. Not a big deal if you're busy."

She smiled as she opened her door. "Tell her I'll be there. I can't resist her cooking."

He waved goodbye as she made the turn to her house. "What do you say we take a walk tonight since we got off a few minutes early?" Gus thumped his tail against the door panel, and Coop could swear he was smiling.

* * *

Coop reviewed the video footage a few times but took a break from work for most of the weekend. Giving his mind a breather often helped him grasp something about a case that eluded him when he was immersed in it. Coop and Gus took advantage of the warmer temperatures and lack of wind over the weekend. They walked their circuit to the park and home both Saturday and Sunday. While Gus explored, Coop analyzed Chandler's case.

When he'd talked with all the scientists on Chandler's team, he didn't get the slightest inkling of guilt from any of them. He recalled Dr. Irene Harris and her excitement and confidence in the new drug. She was the toxicology expert. Her specialty would make her the most qualified in knowing the lethal dose of the drug.

After Camille's Sunday meal, he and AB bantered back and forth about the case. "I'm having a hard time wrapping my head around one of the doctors killing Neil. They're all passionate about the project. The only motive I can come up with is if Neil did something to jeopardize the drug," said Coop.

AB nodded and said, "I can't believe he would do anything to risk the sale and a huge amount of money."

"There are only four people who benefit from Neil's death. His parents, the sister, and Chandler. Chandler had the motive and opportunity. Everything leads back to him," said Coop.

"There has to be another motive we're missing," said AB. "I'll do some more research on his family."

"Unless Chandler did it and he's the best actor·I've ever met," muttered Coop.

* * *

Coop was able to get in an early workout and was at work before seven on Monday. He started a fire and took the chill off the place while Gus perched on his chair and watched.

Coop passed AB coming through the door as he was leaving for Borlund. "I'll be back before lunch," he said.

Coop checked in and made his way to Chandler's office. He found the scientist hunched at his desk in front of a mountain of paperwork and mail. "Hey, Chandler, I've got a few more questions."

"I'm just trying to get through some of the things Neil usually handled. Have you made any progress?" he asked.

"It's slow. I can't seem to come up with a motive. That's why I'm here today. Did you know Dr. Harris has a relative with Alzheimer's?"

He took off his glasses and rubbed his forehead. "I think she mentioned it at the beginning of the project. I don't remember the particulars. Most of us know someone who's been impacted by it. That's one of the reasons we're so enthusiastic about CX-232. We think it will help patients."

"Do you think any of the scientists would steal some of the drug to try it on someone they knew? Like Dr. Harris and her relative?"

Chandler sucked in his breath. "I can't imagine one of them risking our trial and approval by participating in something so unethical."

"Is it possible to see if a person applied to be in the trial and was rejected?"

"I'm afraid it's not. The task of screening candidates is farmed out to a third-party. Our team has nothing to do with selection, to keep everything aboveboard."

Coop nodded. "That makes sense. I'm just trying to connect someone, other than you, to Neil's death."

Chandler sighed. "I appreciate that. I just don't think one of them would do that."

"Did any of them have a close relationship with Neil?"

"Not that I ever saw or knew about."

"Okay, I'll take another run at them and see if I can get anywhere." Coop stood and turned. "One other thing. I talked to Mr. Rusk, the buyer from New York. He's the only one Neil mentioned when he talked to you about selling, is that right?"

"Yes, that's the only deal he discussed with me."

"Did he ever say if he had other offers?"

"Hmm. No, he didn't mention others. I remember when he first talked about it, I got angry and told him I didn't want to sell and didn't want to be bothered by a bunch of companies believing we were trying to sell. It could make it look like we were in trouble with CX-232."

"He told someone he worked with in California about it. Derrick Hudson. Hudson told another colleague, Paul Muller, who is the one who told Mr. Rusk. Do you know any of those people?"

"I may have heard the names, but I don't know them. I've never met them."

"Okay, I'll let you get back to work."

Chandler stepped outside his office to ask Amanda to arrange for Dr. Harris to meet Coop. While he was occupied with Amanda, Coop noticed a legal agreement on his desk. He scanned the transmittal letter from Chandler's corporate attorney. The attorney was providing the necessary forms for removing Neil as an officer of the corporation and a draft of a buyout proposal. It was standard protocol, except for one thing. The attorney referenced Chandler's telephone request for the information— three days before Neil was murdered.

Coop stood and waited for Chandler to return, pondering the significance of yet another piece of evidence implicating his client.

Chandler came through the door, "She's opening the conference room for you and Dr. Harris should be here within thirty minutes."

"Great." Coop took a deep breath. "Chandler, I've got to ask you something." He pointed to the packet from the attorney. "I noticed this. Your attorney drew this up based on your request before Neil's death. Can you explain this?"

Chandler stepped to his desk and looked at the paperwork. "Oh, I probably should have mentioned it before. With all the commotion, I forgot." He slipped into his chair. "I called him after one of our meetings and told him I wanted to get something drawn up to buyout Neil. I thought if I offered him close to what he could get from the offer he was so intent upon accepting, we could end this nonsense and part ways. I'd have to borrow about half of it, but the attorney said that wouldn't be a problem. I could find another partner and only give him a quarter of the company, so I'd have the controlling interest. This was the paperwork for all of that." He took the packet and slid it into a drawer. "It doesn't matter now."

"Actually, it does matter. It gives the police one more thing to add to the pile against you. You no longer have a partner and have sole control, plus a hundred million dollars. All your troubles went away when Neil died."

"But it wasn't like that. I just wanted all the drama of selling the company to end. I knew Neil was fixated on money, so I thought it would solve the issue. I'd have to find somebody who wanted to invest, but the attorney said he could help with that. He didn't think it would be a problem with the promise of CX-232 being a success."

"I've convinced the police to dig deeper into this case. They're probably going to stumble across this, and it will make you look guilty. My advice is to tell them about this. Hiding it would serve to implicate you further."

"That's fine. I didn't kill Neil. I don't have a problem telling the police about this. I never thought about it after Neil's death. That changed everything."

"Exactly. I'll take a copy to Ben, and I suspect they'll want to ask you more about it and talk to your attorney."

"I don't have anything to hide. I didn't do this, Coop."

Amanda made a copy of the documents and Chandler called his attorney and told him he had his permission to discuss their conversations with Coop and the police. Coop stationed himself in the conference room awaiting the arrival of Dr. Harris.

She came through the door, wearing her white lab coat, with a hesitant look of surprise. Coop motioned her to a seat. "Sorry to interrupt you. This should only take a minute. In the course of our investigation, we discovered that your sister-in-law's mother suffers from Alzheimer's."

Her forehead wrinkled. "Yes, yes, Mona has had it for a few years now. That's part of the reason I'm inspired to find a treatment. It's devastating for the whole family."

"Did Mona apply to be in the drug trial?"

"Yes, her doctor submitted her case for consideration."

"But she wasn't chosen?"

Dr. Harris shook her head. "No, I'm afraid she wasn't. We were hopeful, but it didn't happen."

"As you know, Neil was killed with a lethal amount of CX-232, and only a limited number of people had access. I have to ask you, did you take any CX-232 from Borlund Sciences? With your family connection to the disease, it's something we need to consider."

She shook her head. "I understand. Believe me. The family has asked me if there was some way to get Mona access to it. They understand it's experimental and will accept any risks. I would love to be able to help her. I would if I could. I've explained to them we don't have control over the selection process and that she could be chosen for another round of trials." Her lips flattened. "I would never do anything to jeopardize this project. I know it's going to work and I'm hoping Mona is strong enough to be here when it's available for everyone."

"Like I said, not a question I wanted to ask or insinuate, but I had to. I'm very sorry about Mona." He waited a few moments. "Did Neil have much interaction with your team?"

She wrinkled her forehead. "Not much. He stopped in the lab a couple of times a week. Usually, he was looking for Chandler. We heard them talking and arguing about selling the company a few times. We were all in Chandler's court. We liked the way he ran the research team and didn't want to be swallowed up by one of the giants. We all think CX-232 is a good drug and marketable."

"Did Neil try to persuade any of you that selling was a good idea?"

"Not really. He mentioned it a few times. Sort of like a jab at Chandler. None of us took the bait. We all respect Chandler and want to keep advancing in our work. We're all devoted to the field." She paused and added, "We even talked about pooling our resources and buying Neil out, so all the turmoil would end."

"Had you talked to Neil or Chandler about your plan?"

"No, just talk among ourselves. It was something we had been considering, but were too busy to act upon."

Coop bobbed his head in understanding. "Thanks for your time. I'll let you get back to your work."

Coop waved to Amanda as he left and stopped by the cafeteria on his way out of the building. He ran into Bernie, who was in line picking up an early lunch. "Hey, how's it going? Did you solve the case yet?"

Coop grimaced. "No, not yet. Still working on it." He eyed Bernie's tray laden with a huge chef's salad and steaming bowl of soup. "That looks terrific."

"Help yourself. You're on the payroll." Bernie gestured to the trays at the beginning of the line.

"I'm going to grab something on the way back to the office. I need to bring my assistant some lunch."

"Just get something to go for both of you. It's not a problem."

Coop smiled his thanks and scooted to the line. He placed the orders, and a friendly staffer handed him a bag when he got to the end of the line. He looked for a place to pay but didn't see one.

He continued to Bernie's table. "I'm happy to pay, but didn't see a cashier."

"We don't need one. It's all included in our employee package. Don't give it a thought. Guests engaged in business here eat free all the time. If employees get dinners to take home, they just deduct it from our paycheck."

Coop leaned against the table and gestured across the room. "I noticed there's no restricted access to the door to the kitchen. In theory, anyone could get in there, right?"

Bernie nodded. "Yeah, the door is locked at night, but it's open while they're working so they can move back and forth easily."

"We've all but eliminated Jake as a suspect. Neil's soup had to be doctored in the kitchen or the dining room upstairs. I'm curious about visitors the day of the murder. I've checked the lab visitors, but could you send me the access logs for the entire building for that day?"

"Sure thing. I'll get on it when I'm done here."

Chapter 9

Coop put in a call to Ben and told him about the buyout paperwork Chandler had requested from the attorney before Neil's death. He spent the afternoon reviewing the camera footage and studying his notes, looking for clues. He heard the front door and looked out to see the famous brown delivery truck parked at the curb.

Their regular driver was retrieving another load of boxes. Coop, needing a distraction, wandered out to AB's desk. "What do we have here?"

"Oh, I did some online shopping." She gave him a guilty grin. "Shoe sale."

AB had a penchant for shoes. Coop looked down at his worn pair. "I'll never understand women and shoes. I have a dress pair, a pair for the gym, a couple of flip flops for summer and these," he held up his foot, "for winter."

AB was opening her boxes and admiring her new clogs. "Shoes define the person, you know."

Coop laughed and rolled his eyes. He started to walk back to his office and then turned around. "You're a genius, AB."

"Well, thank you for noticing," she said with a laugh. "What do you mean?"

"We need to focus on the shoes in that video footage. I need to get Ben's techs to see if they can enlarge and enhance the floor area.

Maybe the shoes will be more identifiable than the sea of people all dressed alike."

Coop hurried back to his office and put in a call to Ben. Gus elected to stay next to AB's desk and watch her try on her new shoes, sniffing each pair with the thoroughness of a tax auditor.

Ben stopped by right before closing time. Coop handed him a copy of the legal documents related to the buyout and Ben gave Coop a new thumb drive. "Check it out," he said, taking a chair in front of Coop's desk.

Ben read through the paperwork while Coop poured them both a cup of decaf. "I'll add this to the list of incriminating evidence." He raised his eyes to Coop. "Circumstantial, I know. And, he offered it. But he didn't mention it before you found it, so that's a little suspicious."

"I know, one minute I believe he didn't do it and then the next I get this nagging feeling that maybe he did."

Ben smiled. "Well, take a look at what I brought you." Coop loaded the files and studied the screen.

After several minutes, he pointed at the image. "There it is. Everyone is wearing some type of tennis shoe or those clog things," said Coop. He wiggled his brows at Ben, "Except this guy."

Ben smiled. "I knew you'd be excited.

"That shoe is definitely out of place in the kitchen." He stared at the wingtip style dress shoe amid the dozens of more utilitarian styles of footwear expected in a kitchen. "It looks like it has a tassel or that fringed thing on it."

AB stepped into the office and took a look at the image. "That's called a kiltie. It's that fringed piece of leather. I think it does have a tassel as well."

Coop grinned and said, "You're the shoe expert. I'll take your word for it. Good to know your love of shoes proved to be valuable."

Ben chuckled. "I know your next question will be can we identify the body wearing the shoe. The answer is no. We can't see anything because of all the action. We're going to keep searching and see if we can find the shoe elsewhere on camera."

"The shoe eliminates kitchen staff. I'm also going to assume it's a man based on the shoe style. He disguised himself as a kitchen worker by donning one of those shower caps, some gloves, and a white shirt. I saw a bunch of those extra shirts on a rack in the break room. It was too busy for anyone to notice."

Ben stared at Coop's screen. "He's in and out in a matter of minutes, and nobody is the wiser."

"The timestamp on here is eleven-fourteen. We'll need to go over all the video footage for that area with a fine tooth comb."

Ben uttered his agreement and said, "The footage isn't good enough to get a clear image of that shoe. We couldn't use it to pinpoint the actual shoe, but it does point to someone who works in the business or scientific area."

"I guess I'll be spending some time at Borlund roaming the halls and studying shoes." Coop chuckled. "It'll feel like progress compared to what we've had to go on so far."

* * *

The next morning Coop dropped Gus at the office and arrived at Borlund early. He checked in with Bernie and told him he needed to observe and collected a visitor badge. Coop's priority was the CX-232 lab where he wanted to get a good look at the shoes worn by the men on the team.

He stopped by Chandler's office and showed him the photo he had printed from the enhanced footage. "We spotted this out of place shoe in the kitchen near the tray of food the morning of the murder."

Chandler looked down at his shoes, a pair of smooth slip-on loafers. "I usually wear these, but I have a pair like this," he said, pointing to the wingtip.

"Do you recognize this shoe?" asked Coop.

Chandler squinted at the photo and shook his head. "I'm probably the least fashion conscious guy here. I never pay attention to clothes or shoes."

Chandler escorted Coop to the lab. Coop focused his attention on the men. Mac, the computer guru, was wearing black and blue sneakers with jeans under his white lab coat. Dr. Miller was also wearing jeans and brown lace-up shoes.

Coop gave Chandler a wave and headed out to wander the halls and offices of the five-story building. He reconnected with Bernie since he'd most likely need a card to gain entry to many areas. While Bernie printed a list of all the male employees sorted by division, Coop scanned the shoes of the security personnel. They all wore black boots or work style shoes. No fancy tassels or fringed leather.

Coop explained what he was looking for and Bernie vowed to keep it confidential. Bernie suggested he provide a cover for Coop and if asked, he would say he was an insurance inspector. Their first stop was the administration area where most of the business types worked. He ignored offices occupied by women and honed in on the males, ticking off names on the list as he made progress. Coop kept his eyes peeled for the stylish shoe in the photo.

No jeans were worn in this department. Khakis were the most casual attire. Most men wore dress pants with shirts and ties. A prime tasseled wingtip hunting area. Coop nodded and scribbled on his notepad to make it look like he was noting building features. They finished the section, less a couple of employees who were out of the office. Coop had circled three names. All three wore tasseled dress shoes.

They moved on to the legal department next. Coop encountered a mixture of casual and business clad men. Coop circled four more names.

It was close to the lunch hour when they finished, and Bernie suggested a break in the cafeteria. Over another delicious and free meal, they commiserated about the flawed method they were utilizing to locate the shoes. "The problem being many people don't wear the same shoes each day, so we could miss someone who should be on the list," said Coop.

Bernie nodded as he chewed on bites of his sandwich. "The approach of looking through the footage for the day and trying to find someone with the same shoe is probably a better method."

"Yeah, but there's a chance we wouldn't find the guy that way either. We're concentrating on the area around the kitchen when we saw the shoes there."

"Makes sense. Also, check the exit points. The guy had to leave that day. Not sure how much you'll spot, but it's worth a try." He swiped a second napkin. "I'll have the camera operators keep an eye on shoes, and if we spot any like this, we'll get the name of the employee and let you know."

Coop agreed, and after a cursory examination of the gym, daycare, and janitorial areas, he proceeded to the research and scientific support areas. The majority of the men in these departments wore jeans and casual shoes. He found two men wearing dress shoes, but they weren't wingtips.

He handed Bernie his badge and thanked him with a handshake before calling it a day. Bernie promised to email an access report on the circled names to Coop. He thought that would help Coop track them through the building on the day of the murder. Coop stopped at the office, gave AB the circled names to check out, scanned his messages, and picked up Gus.

* * *

Coop and Gus got an early start Wednesday morning. He printed the access report from Bernie for the seven tasseled shoe wearing men and went about reviewing the video footage from the day.

First off, he found Chandler on video and followed him on several cameras to get a good look at his shoes. More bad news. It looked like Chandler's shoes were similar to the image from the kitchen. It was difficult to assess them, but he was confident Ben's techs could work their magic and compare the two.

It was a tedious and tiresome process, broken up by lunch and a walk with Gus to ease his neck and shoulder pain. He spent the entire day searching and viewing and ended up with nothing definitive to implicate any of the men he studied, only another mark against Chandler.

He put in a call to Chandler and asked that he bring in his shoes that were similar to those in the photo he had shown him. Chandler agreed without hesitation and gave no indication of worry or guilt. Coop explained he'd have Ben's techs make some comparisons and with any luck, they might be able to eliminate Chandler if the shoe was not a match.

After his conversation with Chandler, he put in a call to Ben and had to leave a message, but gave him the rundown on Chandler's shoes and asked that he have someone pick them up and analyze them against the video footage.

He turned his attention to the visitors from the logs Bernie had sent but couldn't make out the type of shoes they were wearing. Ben's office would need to enhance the footage to get a better look. He reviewed the list of male employees, striking a few who had been out the day of the murder to eliminate some legwork. He dreaded the thought of combing through hundreds of employees.

AB delivered his mail in the late afternoon, and he saw a letter from his mother with a return address in Vermont. He tapped the envelope on his desk. His eyes burned, accompanied by a dull ache across his forehead. He opted to leave the letter unopened and head home for the evening.

When he arrived at the house, Camille was bustling around the dining room. "Oh, Coop, did you forget I have book club here tonight?"

Coop let out a long sigh and said, "Yeah, I forgot. I'll grab something and get out of your hair."

"You look tired. Did you have a bad day?"

"It was a long, and I made no progress. In fact, the opposite of progress. Just frustrating."

"Mrs. Henderson made a lovely spread. Grab yourself a plate. You're more than welcome to join us. The ladies always enjoy hearing about your work."

He slumped into a chair at the counter while she added grapes to a cheese tray. "I'm not really up to it tonight. Mom sent me a letter from jail today."

Camille stopped her work. "Oh, no. What did she say?"

He shrugged. "Don't know. I decided to wait until I wasn't so tired to deal with it. I can promise you, it won't be good."

"Well, maybe she's had time to think. It could be an apology."

Coop gave her a weak smile. "You are sweet. Naïve, but sweet."

The doorbell rang. "Uh, oh, I'm not quite ready." She pleaded for help with a desperate look on her face.

"All right. I'll get the door and entertain them until you're done."

When Coop opened the door, a handful of Camille's friends poured into the foyer. Eula Mae, Beulah, and Twyla Fay surrounded him. They hugged him and pecked him on the cheek, chattering without letting him get a word in edgewise.

A couple more ladies arrived, and Coop offered to fix them beverages. He delivered a tray of drinks amid questions about his latest case. After giving them a couple of the highlights he excused himself, telling them he had work to do.

While Coop filled a plate with goodies from the buffet, Gus coaxed a few more nibbles from the ladies. Coop gestured, and Gus followed him away from the club meeting to his wing of the house. The dog landed on his chair with a sigh.

Coop settled into his desk and watched video footage from Borlund while he snacked. At Bernie's suggestion, he focused on the exits and honed in on the floor as he watched workers leave the building, hoping to see a tasseled dress shoe.

He scribbled three possible sightings on his notepad. He'd have to visit Borlund to identify the employees and see if they could get a sharper image from their system or have Ben's techs enhance it.

* * *

Thursday Coop spent the day at Borlund getting help with the video footage. Bernie was able to identify the three men Coop found leaving the building the day of the murder. They all worked in administration, and Coop was able to interview them.

All three were cooperative and stunned to learn they were considered to be in the suspect pool. None admitted to having any contact with Neil the day of the murder. None had a personal relationship with Neil, and none had shown up on any footage anywhere near the food tray or kitchen area at the time of the suspected dosing of Neil's food.

Coop pressed them on their relationships with the doctors on the CX-232 team. They all professed to know the scientists, but only in passing. They had never visited the laboratory. They had dropped files in Neil's office as part of their routine duties, but none had been to his office the day of the murder. They all agreed to bring in the shoes they had worn that day for analysis.

He stopped by his office on his way home and gave AB the three names to research. "I don't think they're involved, but want to make sure we exhaust all the possibilities." He retrieved his messages from his desk and palmed the unopened letter from his mother.

After pouring himself a glass of sweet tea, he sunk into the cushions of the couch. Gus hustled to his side and rested his furry head on Coop's knee. Coop tossed the envelope next to him.

He sipped from his glass and rested his head against the plush headrest. "This case is driving me nuts. I can't seem to connect any dots."

"I know. I thought we'd find something in the backgrounds of one of those scientists that would lead us to the killer. Do you still think Chandler is innocent?"

"The evidence is mounting; I'll give you that. He doesn't show any signs of guilt and is very open about cooperating. As dumb as it sounds, I don't think he did it. I'm missing something. Hopefully, it's not that my client is guilty."

"He seemed so upset when he first came to us."

"Yeah, he was. I think he's absorbed in his work. It's his comfort zone, so I'm sure he chooses to focus on it. He's smart enough to know if he's involved the police will prove it. His willingness to share his shoes and the conversation with his lawyer lead me to believe in his innocence."

"The Chandler I remember from school would never harm anyone. I hope he's not guilty."

"Me too, AB. We just need to figure out whatever it is we're missing."

She glanced at the envelope. "I see you haven't opened the letter yet."

He waved it in the air. "How about you open it and read it for me? Just give me the highlights. I'm in no mood for the rantings I suspect are included in here."

He tossed it to AB. She snagged it in midair. "Are you sure?"

He nodded, petting Gus with one hand and sipping from his glass.

She shrugged and slid it open. Coop watched AB's eyes move across the page. Her eyebrows rose several times, and he saw her teeth bite into her bottom lip. She finished the last page and folded it.

"She's upset. Nothing productive in it, just her normal tirade. She can't believe you would leave her in jail. She thinks her lawyer was corrupt and part of the good old boy system in town to make sure she went to jail."

Coop shut his eyes and let out a long sigh. "So, no apology, huh?" He smirked when he asked.

Her lips curved. "Not unless she used invisible ink."

"No surprise there. Aunt Camille thought maybe she was writing to apologize."

"She's a sweetie, but no. Just angry bluster. Maybe Marlene will calm down in a week or so."

"You and Aunt Camille must be members of the Optimist Club. I'm a member of the Realist Club. She's not gonna change. She's a selfish woman only interested in what others can do for her. She's made a mess of her life, and she will never accept responsibility for anything."

"I can't disagree with you. I'm sorry, Coop. Don't let her get to you." She stuffed the envelope into a file folder in her drawer. She grabbed her purse and extended her hand to Coop. "Come on, let's get out of here. Tomorrow will be better."

He heaved himself off the couch and said, "Promise?"

Chapter 10

Coop's Friday morning began with a stack of maple bacon pancakes across from Ben. After they discussed current events and Coop told him about his mom's hate mail, the conversation turned to Chandler's case.

"We picked up Chandler's shoes, and they're working on a comparison. The footage isn't great, so it'll be tough. It doesn't do him any favors, that's for sure. We're having a hard time connecting anyone else with a motive." He finished a bite and added, "I've asked the techs to take a look at the visitor footage you sent my way. Not sure when they'll get to it, but it's on the list."

Coop bobbed his head in agreement. "Got it. It's a long shot. AB and I have been digging into backgrounds and have come up empty."

"All you seem to be uncovering is more evidence against the guy." Ben finished off his last pancake. "I'll concede he's cooperative and his attorney backed up Chandler's version of the conversation about the partnership."

"I don't know what to make of it all. I'll admit the evidence is causing me to doubt him. My gut just says he didn't do it. He couldn't do it. Not the guy we knew."

Ben's cell buzzed, and he ended the call in a hurry and slid out of the booth. "Gotta run. Talk to you later." He waved to Myrtle as he rushed outside and sped away.

"That boy works too hard," said Myrtle, delivering the takeout container and the check.

"Sometimes I think it's a ploy just to get me to buy his breakfast." Coop laughed as he pulled out several bills from his wallet and left them atop the ticket. He slipped his jacket over his t-shirt of the day. White letters declaring, "Don't blame yourself, let me do it," stood out on the navy blue material.

"Y'all have a good day and a nice weekend. Tell AB howdy from me," said Myrtle, gathering the dirty dishes and pocketing the tip.

Coop dropped Gus and AB's breakfast at her desk. He dug into the background reports on those connected to the case. He finished the second one, and his phone rang with a call from Arlo, the Executive Chef at Borlund.

Coop took the call, and after a short conversation told AB he was heading to Borlund. He tossed his notepad and working file on the seat of the Jeep and rushed through the streets.

He checked in at the desk and retrieved a visitor badge before making his way to the cafeteria. He found Arlo in his office with Marco, the missing kitchen staffer who had been on a cruise until today.

Arlo shut the door and the threesome wedged into the small space. The Executive Chef introduced Coop and said, "Marco just got back to work today, and we were filling him in on the death of Mr. Borden. When he left, we had no idea it was murder. Anyway, Marco remembered something, and I thought we should call you as you said."

Coop gave an enthusiastic nod. "Yes, I've eliminated several leads so new information would be great. What is it you remember?"

Marco said, "I was just telling Chef that I remember something sort of weird that morning. I saw the tray set up like it always is. We have small nameplates we use for Mr. Hollund and Mr. Borden.

They each have different foods they like, so we put the little sign next to their plate. That way they get the salad dressing they like and stuff like that."

Coop gestured his understanding. "Got it, that makes sense."

"Anyway, I noticed that someone had added cilantro on the top of Mr. Hollund's soup."

"I take it that was a problem?"

Marco and Arlo both nodded. "Mr. Hollund hates cilantro. We always substitute parsley for him. I figured whoever put it on the tray just put it on the wrong side. I switched the nameplates so Mr. Borden would get the soup with the cilantro and Mr. Hollund would get the parsley."

Coop's forehead furrowed. "Okay, so the soups were changed here in the kitchen. What time was this?"

"Hmm," said Marco. "I changed them right before Jake came with the plates. Then he took off, so it was right before he left with the tray. I was glad I caught it."

"Do you know who messed up the soups when they were placed on the tray?"

Arlo said, "From my interviews with staff that next day, it was Nick. He's a kitchen assistant. At the time we didn't know about the misplacement. All he did was take the bowls to the tray after Zach filled them."

"Right. I appreciate the information. Let's see if Nick remembers anything or seeing anyone by the tray when he placed the soup. I don't want to draw too much attention. Do you think you can talk to Nick without raising any eyebrows?"

Arlo gave a confident nod. "Sure thing."

"I need to get back on the line," said Marco. "Do you need anything else from me?"

Coop extended his hand, "Thanks, Marco, you've been a big

help. I'll look into this, and if I need more information, I'll be in touch. Please just keep this all confidential."

"I understand. I won't say a word. I'm still in shock Mr. Borden was murdered."

Coop waited for Marco to leave and then shut the door. "I've got an image I want you to look at and tell me what you think. It's taken from the camera in the kitchen, and it's not great, but shows someone wearing dress shoes next to the tray of food. We think someone came into the kitchen and doctored the soup when it was on the tray."

He slid the photo across the desk and Arlo squinted at it. "I don't know who it is, but I can tell you it's not one of my staff members. We don't allow that type of shoe. Everyone has to wear slip resistant shoes."

"You don't recognize the shoes or anything else?"

Arlo shook his head. "I'm afraid not."

"Is it feasible that someone could sneak in and out unnoticed? You'll see from the photo of the cart area how everyone looks the same. White shirts like all your staff wear and the shower cap things on their heads. We didn't notice anything until we focused on the shoes."

"Wow. I'd like to think we would notice an outsider, but it's obvious we didn't. It's a busy time in the kitchen with people moving around. We've never given security a thought. Our whole focus is on making sure we have lunch ready. It's our busiest time of the day. If he slipped in and out, we probably wouldn't notice anything unless he did something to draw our attention."

Coop nodded. "Yeah, that's what we thought." He slid the photos back in his file. "We need to keep this quiet. I don't want anyone tipping our guy off that we have a good lead."

"I won't say anything. I'll see if Nick can tell us anything more.

There's nothing to make me suspect he would be involved. I think he probably didn't pay attention when he put the soups on the tray."

"Makes sense. Not a big deal on any other day. Just get back to me when you know anything. I'll also need a copy of both of their files so we can do a background on them." Coop stood and added, "I'll be in the building a bit longer. Just call my cell if you get it figured out."

Arlo promised to have copies of their files sent to Amanda within the hour. Coop left the kitchen and made his way to Chandler's office. He was in the lab, so Coop waited while Amanda got in touch with him. As he sat waiting, the latest information from Marco tumbled through his mind like clothes in a dryer. *So our killer got the wrong guy. I wonder if he'll try again.*

Chandler arrived and greeted Coop with, "What's new?"

"I just came from the kitchen where I learned some new information." Coop explained what Marco had told him. He watched as the realization hit Chandler.

Chandler stammered as he said, "Uh, so, you think the lethal dose was meant for me?"

Coop's head tipped in a slow nod. "Yeah, that's what I've been contemplating. I'll look into Marco and see if there's anything that would tie him to this, but my gut says no. He could have played dumb and not said anything if he was the killer."

Chandler's hand went to his forehead. "Now we need to figure out who would want me dead?"

"It's a working theory at this point, but yes. Arlo and Marco know about the soup mistake, but I'll leave it up to you if you want to include your security department. I wanted you to be alert and mull over anyone with a motive. Again, the list of suspects is limited to the people who would have access to CX-232." He paused and added, "Or could have been convinced to access if for someone else."

Chandler shook his head back and forth several times. "Nobody on my team would do this. I didn't think they were capable of killing Neil and I certainly don't think they would kill me." He stood and paced around the conference table. "This is crazy."

"Is there any way a competitor could have gotten hold of CX-232?"

He lips formed a thin line. "I can't fathom a way."

"Who would benefit from your death?"

"Outside of some charitable donations, I've left everything to my parents and if they're gone to my siblings. I don't have a wife or kids."

"How's your relationship with your family?"

"I don't see them much." He dropped into a chair. "Amanda mentioned yesterday that we do get some threatening emails and letters every so often. She thought there could be a motive in there. Usually, they're from a family member of someone taking one of our drugs who has died or has an adverse side effect. The lawyers told us not to respond to those. Maybe we need to look through them and see if there is anything of value?"

"I'll do that. Nothing stood out and made you nervous from those letters?"

He shrugged. "It made me feel bad, but not nervous. I don't remember anyone threatening death, just legal action. I got into this business to help people, not hurt them. I know there's a risk with any drug, but I like to think the benefit far outweighs the risk. I would never intentionally put a product out that I knew would harm people, no matter how much money I could make. I left it up to Amanda to alert me to anything I should know. Neil probably has some of the same types of letters." Chandler pushed a button on his phone and asked Amanda to retrieve the file.

Coop scribbled on his notepad. "We'll go through your file, and

I'll check with Melissa before I leave."

After a quick knock on the door, Amanda came through with a file folder and placed it on the conference table. Chandler rifled through the papers and scanned each document. She handed Coop the personnel files he had requested from Arlo.

While he was reading, Coop's cell rang out. Arlo was on the line to report his findings. Coop penned notes in his file and thanked him before disconnecting. "Arlo said he's sure the soup placement was an oversight. Nick wasn't paying close attention. Didn't know the difference between parsley and cilantro. Marco changed it when he saw it and never said anything. Arlo is convinced it was an honest mistake. I'll look into it, but tend to agree."

"I've never had any issues with anyone on the kitchen staff. Honestly, I can't remember having a problem with anyone here at work. Well, really with anyone. I can't imagine who would want to harm me." He took off his glasses and rubbed the bridge of his nose. "And Neil's death is on my conscious now. He died because he got my soup."

"Don't blame yourself for that. Only the killer is to blame. We need to concentrate on figuring out how the killer got access to CX-232." Coop took another sheet of paper from his file. "These three guys were seen the day of Neil's murder wearing shoes like those I showed you before. Do any of them cause you any concern? Do you know any of them?"

Chandler scanned the list. "I know they work in Admin. If I remember, they work with contracts and compliance."

"That's correct. I talked to all of them and we're running their backgrounds, but nothing came up to indicate they would be involved in a murder. No financial concerns or windfalls. No access to the lab. No visits to the lab."

Chandler continued to shake his head. "I can't think of any

difficulties we've had with any of these men." He handed Coop the file of complaints and said, "I read through these, and most of the threats are pretty veiled. A couple of them mention they hope I die the same way their loved ones did, by poisoning myself with my own medicine. I wrote it off to grief and anger. I understand they're upset."

Coop took the file. "We'll check them out, just the same. The mention of poisoning is a red flag. You need to be on guard now that we know you were the likely target. Do you have a security system at home?"

He nodded and said, "Yeah. I guess I better start making sure I use it all the time. I'm not good about it. I'm going to let Bernie know about the theory. I have complete faith in him."

"That's good. I'm glad you can trust him. Stay alert and use the alarm system."

"I think I'll start going out for lunch," he said, with a slight chuckle that didn't do much to mask his unease.

"Might be a good idea until we get this resolved." Coop stood to leave. "Remember, you can call if you have any problems. Day or night, my cell is always on."

Coop stopped by Neil's office and asked Melissa for any threatening emails or letters she had collected for Neil. "Oh, we funneled all of those to Chandler's office. He had already started collecting them, so we sent along anything we received here. Most of them seemed harmless. I think they were seeking money more than anything else." She paused and added, "Do you think that has something to do with Neil's death?"

"Not sure. Just looking at all the angles."

* * *

Coop and AB spent the rest of the afternoon going through the file of threatening letters and emails. AB ran an extensive background report on Marco and Nick, the kitchen assistant who mishandled the soup.

Their personnel files were unremarkable. Neither had ever been in any trouble. Nick had a satisfactory review and had only been there for a year. Marco had glowing reviews and had been promoted throughout the years.

AB reviewed their financials and took a cursory look at social media profiles. "No indication either of them was paid to drug the soup. They don't live above their means and no posts or jokes about being unhappy at work."

"Let's see if we can connect any of the hate mail in Chandler's file with any employees of Borlund. Maybe somebody is playing the long game and infiltrated." He took a look at his notepad and added, "Also, let's do the same with the male visitors the day of the murder. I can't make out their shoes and want to check them out for possible ties."

"That's going to take some time, but I'll get started. I'll have Madison and Ross help."

Coop looked at the time. "Ben's on his way. I told him I had some new information. It's late. Enjoy your weekend, AB. We can hit this hard starting on Monday."

She gathered her things and gave Gus a nuzzle before leaving. As she was opening her door, Ben pulled into the lot behind the office. "He's waiting for you," she hollered as she waved goodbye.

Ben, toting takeout bags from a Chinese restaurant, came through the back door and shouted out a greeting. Gus came barreling around the corner, his nose in the air, following the scent of egg rolls and sesame chicken.

Coop joined him in the kitchen and over heaping plates of their favorite selections shared the latest on the soup swap at Borlund. He outlined what he knew and told him about the collection of threatening mail Chandler had collected. "I'm not sure it's even connected, but we're looking into it. Since our mystery man doctored the soup intended for Chandler, I'm betting he was the target."

Ben choked on his food and guzzled a long drink from his cup. "Our guy got the wrong guy. That's a twist I didn't see coming. I'll have Kate and Jimmy get started on looking at it from that angle Monday." He took another forkful of rice. "I wonder who would want Chandler dead."

Chapter 11

Sunday evening Coop's phone played the theme from *Perry Mason*, announcing a call from Ben. "Hey Coop, I'm at the ER with Chandler."

"What happened?"

"He was out for a run and almost got taken out by a car. He wanted me to call you. Said it might be related to the latest theory about the poisoning."

"I'll be right there." He left Gus with Aunt Camille and dashed the few blocks to the hospital. He shuddered when he walked through the glass doors. He hated hospitals, and the memory of his emergency trip through the same doors was fresh in his mind.

He was directed to a treatment room and found Ben outside the door. "What do you think?"

"Can't know for sure. He was jogging near his home. No street cameras in the area. It was almost dark. He says he heard an engine rev and had to take evasive action to get out of its way. He's got a lot of road rash, a severely sprained ankle, and a broken wrist."

Coop grimaced. "No leads at all?"

"None. We're scanning road cameras on the main streets coming out of his neighborhood and looking for any home security camera footage, but so far we've got zilch. All he knows is it was a dark sedan. He's not what you call a car guy, so no clue on the make."

"Okay if I go in and see him for a few minutes?"

"Sure, he gave his statement. I told him we'd give him a ride home, but you can do that if you want."

"Yeah, I'll take him home. Maybe he can stay somewhere until we get this sorted."

Ben gave him a wave and joined two of the patrol officers who had been on the scene of Chandler's accident.

Coop tapped on the glass door, and Chandler motioned him inside. "Hey, Chandler. How are ya feeling?" He took in the cast on his client's wrist and the scrapes on his arms and face. His running pants were ripped and strewn across the bed. Blood from the fresh abrasion on his right knee trailed down his calf ending at the wrapping covering his ankle. His left knee was scraped raw. "Scared, shaky, and lucky. Thanks for coming. Ben said he was going to call you."

"Yeah, I just talked to him. I told him I'd give you a ride home when they spring you."

"I'm waiting on the nurse to come back and check on me. Doc just left and said no concussion."

"Ben said you don't remember much about the car, just that it was dark. Did it have its lights on?"

"No, it didn't. I didn't see it at all until it was right up on me. I just heard it and looked behind me, and there it was. I had to dodge it and tripped on the curb and fell on my knees. Apparently, my wrist took the brunt." He held up his arm. "This is a serious inconvenience."

"Are you going to be okay at your place? Is there somewhere else you can go until this is all resolved?"

"I could go to a hotel, I guess." He rested his head against the pillows behind him. "I'd rather be at home. Do you think I need better security?"

"I'm not sure. Do you have cameras installed at your house?"

He shook his head. "No, just the alarm."

"You might want to consider cameras. You can monitor them from your phone when you're away. I can give you the name of a reputable installer."

"That sounds like a good suggestion. If he could start on that tomorrow, that would be great."

Coop nodded and tapped the buttons on his phone. "I just sent him a text. Trevor's a good guy, and I told him you were in a hurry. I'm sure he'll be in touch first thing in the morning." Coop slipped his phone back in his pocket. "Are you set up to work from home? Could you take some time off and lay low?"

"The way I'm feeling right now, I'll need to take a few days off. I can do some work at home. Nothing related to the files associated with CX-232. Those are locked down, but as I said, I'm transitioning to a new project. I could use the time to think."

"What are you going to do about a business partner?"

"Now that I don't need to find an investor. I've been toying with the idea of hiring a top-notch business manager. That way I could retain a hundred percent ownership of the company. I don't want to get in a hurry to find someone and then have it not be a good match."

Coop nodded. "That sounds like a good option. Better to take your time with such an important decision."

"The insurance money is tied up until this whole investigation is concluded. That's frustrating, but I know it will work out in the end."

"We've been banging our heads on the proverbial rock trying to figure out who would benefit from your death. There's nothing to indicate your family would cause you harm. None of the doctors on your team have a motive. You don't have any romantic problems, right?"

Chandler shrugged. "No, sadly, I don't have much of a personal life. I am way too focused on work. That's why my marriage didn't work."

"What about your ex-wife? Does she get anything in the event of your death?"

He shook his head. "No, we split up long before my success, and it was a pretty simple divorce. No kids, no big assets. We both walked away. It was amicable."

"No hidden past? Affairs? Kids you don't know about?"

He smirked and the corners of his lips lifted. "No, I'm not that exciting. No real relationships. The last date I went on was years ago. Nothing long term. I'm pretty much a workaholic."

"I saw in your personnel handbook that employees working with confidential and corporate secrets are subject to random polygraph screening. How would you feel about having your team polygraphed?"

"Oh, wow. That would be a first. Under the circumstances, I'm sure they would understand. Probably wouldn't be overjoyed, but I can't imagine they would be uncooperative."

"I'll set that up with your human resources people. I'm grasping at straws, but am beginning to wonder if one of them isn't being bribed or used in some way."

Their conversation was interrupted by a nurse who applied bandages to the most severe lacerations. She had discharge papers with her and Chandler signed them as best he could with his left hand.

Coop helped him into the Jeep and drove him to his home in the neighborhood bordering Belle Meade. Coop gave him a hand up the steps and got him settled downstairs. Once he had Chandler dosed with his medications and everything within his reach, Coop took a cursory look around the exterior of the house. It was on a cul-de-sac and fenced, but not a fortress, by any means. After checking to make sure all the entry points were secure he went back inside. "I'll check on you tomorrow. Give a call if you need anything. I'm not that far away." Coop made sure the alarm was activated when he left.

* * *

Monday Coop stopped by Chandler's house and delivered coffee and pastries. Trevor had already been in contact with Chandler and would be upgrading his system and installing cameras for him. Coop sat for a few minutes sipping his coffee, taking in the vivid bruises and marks across his client's body.

"You look like you lost a fight. How are ya feeling?"

"Sore. Everywhere," Chandler said, tipping up his cup with an awkward motion of his left hand.

"If you need any items from work or errands or anything, we can deliver for you."

Chandler offered Coop a weak smile. "That's kind of you. I appreciate all you've done." He struggled to put the cup on the side table. "I don't have a large circle of friends."

"I've only got two, but they're the best. I can count on Ben and AB for anything. Plus I've got my aunt. I'd be lost without them."

"You're lucky, Coop. I've been sitting here alone all night and realize I need to build a life outside of my work. I need to do a better job of staying in touch with my family. I called my parents last night."

"That sounds like a good start. Maybe a little time off will do you some good."

"This is probably the first time in my life I haven't gone to work. I'm rarely sick and tend to go in no matter what. The way I feel right now, I just want to sit here and not move."

Coop chuckled. "I hear ya. Just don't stay still too long or you won't be able to move later. It's better to walk around a bit. You've got your crutches and the walker if you need them."

"Yeah, I've been using the walker for short trips. Makes me feel like an invalid. I need to find some movies to watch, or I'm going to go crazy. My head's too fuzzy to think too hard, so I'm going to rest for the day."

"Give a holler if you want some food delivered. I'm a master at takeout." Coop gave him a wave and ran into Trevor as he was leaving. He followed him inside for an introduction and slipped away while Chandler explained the finer points of his property.

Coop drove to the West Precinct to meet Ben. Gus followed Coop and delayed his arrival in Ben's office due to excessive petting from the detectives who knew him. Ben was on the phone, as usual. Coop finished his coffee and waited.

When Ben hung up, he said, "Any updates?"

"Not really. I talked to Chandler last night and stopped by this morning. He's pretty banged up. I told him I wanted to arrange for polygraphs for the doctors on his team."

Ben's brows arched. "That might rattle a cage or two."

"That's what I thought. I'm on my way to talk to somebody at Borlund about coordinating them. Chandler says they've never done it before, although it's part of their employment agreement."

"I was just checking to see if we had any news from the Caymans." He shook his head with disgust. "Nothing. The burner phone we found in Neil's car only called one other number. Another burner phone."

"Any chance of tracing it?"

"So far a dead end. The area code is from Washington, but that doesn't mean much. The phone is inactive at the moment and hasn't been used since the last time it connected with Neil's. We're working on tracing where it was purchased."

"The ex-wife lives in Seattle. There could be a connection. I'll get in touch with her and see what she can tell us."

Ben nodded. "Good idea. We pulled her phone and credit, but didn't see anything to indicate any contact or travel."

"Maybe she hired someone. I'll give it a shot and let you know if I come up with anything worthy of a follow-up," offered Coop.

"Sounds good. That would be a big break if we could get somewhere with one of these leads."

"I've got the file with all the emails from Borlund. That's going to take some serious time to go through." Coop rolled his eyes. "I'm not sure it will be worth the effort."

"Send the files over, and we'll see what the techs can do to speed up the search. They can program it to look for keywords, rather than a manual search."

"Will do. Chandler's got Trevor over at his house upgrading his security and putting in cameras. Just to be on the safe side."

"Whatever is going on has to be connected to the company. The sale. The new drug," said Ben.

"I'm going to request to observe the polygraphs, and in the meantime, I'll keep going through camera footage. I'd like to find those exact shoes the day of the murder."

"The techs are still checking Chandler's shoes. The quality of the footage isn't great."

"After talking to the guys who were wearing that type of shoe on the day of the murder, I don't think they have anything to do with it, but we're checking them for ties to the scientific team."

"Maybe the polygraphs or threat of them will cut something loose."

"That's what I'm hoping. I'll keep you in the loop."

* * *

Although the theory of Chandler being the target was upmost in Coop's mind, he needed to exhaust the leads relating to Neil. His burner phone calling one with a Washington area code could be a link to the ex-wife. Tuesday AB got in touch with Neil's ex-wife, Carol, and set up a late afternoon video meeting for Coop. When the call connected, Coop saw a dark-haired woman on his screen. Carol worked in advertising and was calling from her office. Coop thanked her for taking time to talk to him.

"I'm happy to help. I was stunned to hear Neil had died. This is the first I've heard that there's a murder investigation. I can't believe it."

"When was the last time Neil was in contact with you?"

"Oh, wow. It's been years. We've been divorced for over twenty years. We got married too young, and it just didn't work. We didn't think it through. We were both in college and thought we were soulmates. I used to hear from him when he was still living in California, but I haven't talked to him since he moved."

He then asked her if she recognized the phone number from the burner phone. She shook her head and said, "No, that's not familiar at all."

"Do you know of anyone who would want to harm Neil? Did he have an ongoing feud or issue with anyone from the past?"

Carol didn't know anyone from Neil's past who would be holding a grudge against him. She couldn't think of anyone who had been at odds with Neil from their time together.

"Did he have friends or know people in Washington outside of you?"

The woman's forehead wrinkled in thought. "I can't think of anyone he had a relationship with here. It's been so long though; he could have had friends here I didn't know anything about."

"He never mentioned visiting Washington or looked you up when he attended a conference there?"

She shook her head again. "No, I never had a visit from him, and he never mentioned attending any conferences here. The last time we talked was when he said he was leaving California for a job in Nashville."

"Do you know his partner, Chandler Hollund?"

She shook her head. "No, I've never met him. I've never visited Nashville."

"You had no children together, correct?"

"That's right. I remarried about fifteen years ago and have two children with my husband."

"How would you characterize your divorce?" he asked.

"Oh, it was simple and polite. We didn't have much and went our separate ways. We were renting an apartment, so no real assets. He had a car, and I had a car. We split the household stuff, and that was that. My parents lived up here, so I moved back and started over."

"Did Neil get along with his family? Were they close?"

"His parents were always courteous, but not involved. Neil was never super close to his family. They didn't seem like the close-knit type. He had a sister, and I know she had a son. Last I knew she was divorced and the son was in and out of trouble, but it's been a long time."

"If you think of anything else or run across anything that relates to Neil, please get in touch with me." He gave her his cell phone number and thanked her again before disconnecting the call.

He wandered out to the reception area as AB was turning off her computer. "Any luck?" she asked.

"Nope. She hasn't talked to Neil since he moved out here. I don't think she's lying. She never met Chandler. Ben can dig into her and check her out, but I think it's a dead end. I'm banking on the polygraphs to rattle our doctors. I half expected the threat of them would cause someone to come forward today."

* * *

The polygraph examinations were scheduled for first thing Wednesday morning. The examiner was a seasoned professional Coop had worked with on prior cases. The exams were conducted at an office building on the Vanderbilt campus.

Coop was behind a glass window where he could watch the proceedings. The results were transmitted to the examiner's computer, and a computer in the room Coop occupied behind the one-way glass.

Coop had met with Harry, the examiner, on Tuesday and summarized what he was hoping to learn from the examinations. With Coop's help, Harry composed a series of questions that would be used for all the scientists.

Harry worked through the team members and asked mundane questions before getting into the meat of the examination. Coop observed the first exam noting Dr. Devi was calm throughout the proceedings. She remained unemotional when asked if she had ever removed CX-232 from the secure lab. A spark of uncertainty flashed in her eye when she was asked about being forced to access the drug on behalf of someone else. Harry pressed on and asked if she had been coerced or blackmailed to gain access to the drug. It was clear she had expected the questions related to her work and any unauthorized removal of the drug or sale of the drug, but the look on her face broadcast the fact that she was surprised at the questions centered on personal duress.

Mac, the computer scientist, was next in the chair. Coop noted his relaxed demeanor when he had interviewed him at Borlund, and he gave the same nonchalant appearance when Harry began the examination. His forehead wrinkled when Harry got to the coercion questions, but Mac continued in his laid-back voice.

Dr. Swenson came into the room exhibiting nervousness. Beads of sweat glistened above her lip, and her tongue darted out to moisten her dry lips, as Harry connected the monitors. She calmed a bit when he asked the routine questions and settled into a rhythm.

Dr. Harris arrived and carried on a polite banter with Harry before the questioning began. She appeared confident and didn't falter when asked about coercion. She had been forthcoming with Coop about her relative's diagnosis and didn't seem as put off about the questions as the others. Coop scribbled a note to remind Harry she was the team member Coop had questioned a second time due to her family dealing with Alzheimer's.

Dr. Miller was the last appointment before their lunch break. Coop checked his shoes but discovered he was wearing the brown lace-up style he had been wearing before. He was a somber guy and didn't make small talk. He answered the questions in a mechanical way and gave no indication of surprise when the questions about bribery or duress were asked.

When his examination was complete, Coop read through the notes he had scribbled and waited for Harry. As soon as Dr. Miller left, Harry came through the door. "Ready for a lunch break, Coop?"

"Beyond ready. I'll meet you back here at two-thirty. I'm going to grab lunch and take it to Chandler, and then I'll bring him back for his test." Coop stopped at a deli and picked up lunch. He found Chandler dressed and waiting. Trevor was fine-tuning the camera system and showing Chandler how to monitor them on his phone.

After a quick lunch, Coop drove Chandler to the campus and helped him get inside the building. Harry hooked up the monitors and began his questions. Chandler answered without any hesitation and remained composed and calm throughout the process.

Once he was done, Harry packed up his gear and promised to email his report in the morning. Coop dropped Chandler at his house and picked up Gus from the office. He left his notepad on his desk with two names circled. Two of the doctors on Chandler's team had answered yes to being asked about gaining access to the drug known as CX-232. One was Dr. Harris, and the other was a surprise.

Chapter 12

The staff at Harrington and Associates spent Thursday morning immersed in research, checking social media connections between the hate mailers and the scientists. They were diving into the backgrounds of the visitors and looking for ties between them and any of the scientists.

Coop's conference table was covered with files and paperwork. He moved the folders he was confident in eliminating to a pile on his credenza. The kitchen staff made up the most significant portion of the cleared files. He also moved Melissa's, Neil's assistant, to the credenza.

Coop took a break and refilled his cup in the kitchen, splashing a bit of coffee on his humorous t-shirt. His "Be happy I'm not a twin" shirt was dark brown. Coop blotted at the spots, thankful it wasn't one of his white t-shirts. Although he had dozens in his collection, he was protective of them. The last time he kept wearing one with holes, AB prodded him for weeks to get rid of it. She only convinced him after she scoured the Internet for days and found a replacement.

While he was dabbing at his shirt, AB hollered from her desk. "Harry just emailed his report. I'll leave it on your desk."

Coop grabbed a snickerdoodle from the plate on the table and darted to his office. He scanned the report, flipping through the standard disclaimers and getting to the heart of the analysis. Harry provided a separate report on each examinee and an overall summary. In his opinion, there was no deception indicated on the part of Chandler or his team members. He noted reactions to the questions about coercion were most likely surprise and based on the scoring he used to evaluate responses none of them were lying.

Dr. Devi had been the other doctor who indicated she had been asked about obtaining the new drug. She was asked a follow-up question about taking any action based upon the request and had answered in the negative. She also gave no indication of deceit when asked about removing the drug from the secure lab.

Coop wanted to share the information with Chandler before he talked to Dr. Devi. AB came through his office door. "I just finished reading it. What do you make of Dr. Devi's response?"

"Not sure. We'll have to talk to her and probe into her answer a bit."

"I sent a copy to Ben, so he'll be aware of it."

"How are you doing on research?"

"We're not even close to being done. I think it will take several more days to go through it."

"I'll run over to Chandler's and then probably make a stop at Borlund to get to the bottom of Dr. Devi's answer. I'll leave Gus here for the day."

* * *

Still in a robe, Chandler greeted Coop and led him to the living room. "Dr. Devi has been texting me and calling me all morning. She said she needs to explain something before I get the polygraph report."

Coop accepted a cup of coffee and when he took the first sip could tell it was caffeinated. He let the forbidden liquid linger in his mouth before swallowing. He eyed the standard-sized cup, rationalizing it was only a few more tablespoons than he had allotted himself each day.

"That's why I'm here. I wanted to let you know what we learned and get your take." He showed Chandler the report and explained Dr. Devi had shown a reaction to the questions about being asked to obtain CX-232, but there was no indication that she had removed any of it from the secure lab.

"Shall I call her and see what she says?"

"If you're comfortable. I could go meet with her, if you prefer."

Chandler squeezed his temples. "I've never doubted anyone on the team. I'm just at a loss."

Coop nodded. "Let me go talk to her and get some answers. I'll tell her you're not feeling well and asked me to intervene."

Chandler sank back into the recliner he was sitting in and sighed. "That's probably best. I'm beginning to doubt my ability to judge people."

Coop spent time visiting with Chandler, distracting him from the current circumstances and fetching a few things for him. After he had the patient situated with snacks and a series he recommended Chandler watch, he took off for Borlund.

Assuming Dr. Devi would be in the lab, he asked Amanda if he could use Chandler's conference room. She located Dr. Devi, who arrived within minutes.

Her eyes were wide and tired. He offered her a chair and said, "Chandler received your texts. I just visited with him this morning, and he's not up to a conversation today."

Her head bobbed in understanding. "I need to explain something to him. I wanted to contact him before he received a report from the examinations."

"He asked that I talk with you. I've also been given a copy of the report from yesterday."

Her shoulders slumped. "I was truthful when I answered the questions. I know we have to answer yes or no and can't offer any clarification. I wanted Dr. Hollund to understand why I answered yes to being asked about obtaining CX-232."

"The examiner's findings indicate no deception on your part. He believed you were truthful in your answers. I'm happy to hear your explanation and relay that information to Chandler. He's trying to rest and get stronger so he can be back at work soon."

"Yes, yes. We would all like him to be back at work. I don't want him to doubt my loyalty to him or our project. I am from India, as is my husband. We still have family there. We are both doctors. Many of our immediate family members live here in America, but I have an uncle still living in India. He has several children and grandchildren. One, in particular, is not hard working or successful. He's a hoodlum. Always asking for money and thinks he deserves more."

She rotated one of the shiny bracelets she wore on her wrist. "My father talks to my uncle, and he likes to talk about our lives here in America. He tends to brag about our successes."

"At the end of summer I received a call from Ranjan, he's my distant cousin. He demanded that I procure some of the drugs we have developed and any in development and bring them to India so he could sell them to people who want to make counterfeit medicines." She shook her head with despair. "Ranjan lives with others like him. They make their living not by working, but by stealing and threatening people. They've taken tourists from the streets and demanded money for their safe return."

She shook her head. "I, of course, told him no. I would not steal anything for him and that what he was doing was wrong. He said my uncle and aunt, his great-grandparents, would be hurt if I didn't do this for him." She took a long breath. "Ranjan told me the thugs he runs with would do horrible things."

Coop asked, "Did anything happen to your uncle or his family?"

She shook her head. "No. I called my father and told him he had to talk to his brother and explain Ranjan's horrible scheme and his criminal entanglements. My father and I sent money to them so they could go away quickly. My father has been trying to convince my uncle to turn Ranjan into the police."

Coop asked her for the date of the call and transfer of funds and her father's name and contact information, along with the complete names of her uncle and cousin. He jotted notes as she recalled facts and recited her savings account number.

He studied her face and saw the fear and sadness in her eyes. "I'm sorry for your family. I'm sure it's stressful and hard for you." She nodded with tears threatening. "Just to be clear that is the only time you've been asked to procure CX-232 from Borlund?"

She frowned. "Yes, yes. That is the only time. I knew it wasn't relevant to the poisoning of Mr. Borden, but I wanted to be truthful."

"And you never reported this incident with your family to anyone here at work?"

She cast her eyes downward and shook her head. "No," she whispered. "I was ashamed. Ranjan is a disgrace. That is not what my family is like. We are hard workers and honest people."

"I understand. I'll let Chandler know the circumstances. You were right to answer truthfully."

"We are waiting for word from my uncle. He finally agreed to contact the police, but he fears they will have to leave the town where they live. They won't be safe from Ranjan's friends. My father has offered to help them relocate."

Coop stood and opened the door for Dr. Devi. "I hope things work out for your uncle and his family. Again, I'm sorry for your trouble."

He followed her out and thanked Amanda before heading back to the office. Gus greeted him at the door with a frenzy of tail wagging. Coop found AB seated at the conference table surrounded by reports and files.

"Well, how did it go?" she asked.

"She had a plausible explanation for her answers. Could you pull her financial report and let me take a look at it? I need bank statements for the savings account." While AB shuffled through folders, he told her about Dr. Devi's distant cousin and his extortion attempts.

AB scurried to her desk and returned with a report. "I didn't have the savings account. It's in her husband's name." She flipped through the pages and ran her finger down a list of transactions. "Here's a transfer to an account at the same bank at the end of August." She spelled the last name of the account holder.

He nodded. "That's her father. So, it checks out."

"Now we're back to square one," she said, blowing her bangs out of her eyes.

* * *

Friday morning Coop received a text from AB, saying she was sick and staying home for the day. Coop arrived at Peg's before Ben. He savored the robust and warm beverage he craved like oxygen while he waited.

He let Myrtle top off his coffee as Ben walked through the door. "Hey, sorry I'm late. The kids couldn't find their homework." He reached for the sugar shaker. "It's going to be one of those days."

"Yeah, AB is out sick today."

"Uh, oh. That means you'll be without adult supervision today." Ben laughed as Myrtle arrived to take their orders.

"Have y'all decided," she asked. "We've got those crepes AB like so much."

"She's home not feeling well today."

"Oh, that poor dear. I'll put in an order for some chicken soup, and you can drop that off for her." She finished taking their orders and left them to solve the problems of the world at their weekly breakfast meeting.

"We dug into the ex-wife and can't find anything to link her to the burner phone or Neil. I think she's clean," said Ben.

"I'm not surprised. She didn't give any signs of deception when we talked online." He shook his head in disgust. "We just keep hitting one brick wall after another."

Coop explained the results of the polygraph exams and Dr. Devi's situation before Myrtle arrived with their breakfast platters. "I won't be making much headway on Chandler's case today. With AB gone, I've got to do a couple of reports for a divorce case and a worker's compensation fraud. Is the DA pressuring you to turn over the case yet?"

Ben wiped his mouth and shook his head. "Nah, not yet. I'm not confident we could make a case stick against Chandler. He's our best suspect, but you've uncovered enough concerns to raise doubt. It's not a winner of a case at this point."

"That's a relief. I'd like to get to the bottom of it, so I can focus on some other work."

Myrtle returned with a bag of takeout containers. "There's enough soup in here to get AB through the weekend. I put in a few biscuits in case she needs somethin' more substantial. You tell her I hope she feels better."

"I'll do that. Thank you for suggesting the soup." He took the check from her.

"You behave today. Without that girl to watch over y'all, there's no tellin' the trouble y'all will find." She gave him a wink.

Ben smirked, and Coop said, "Why does everybody think I can't manage on my own?"

Ben motioned to Coop's chest sporting "I work well with others, as long as they leave me alone" across his green t-shirt.

"You're just jealous of my collection. Admit it."

Ben followed Coop to his Jeep and slipped Gus a wedge of pancake he had wrapped in a napkin for him. "Aww, poor guy. You'll probably starve without AB there today." He gave Coop a crooked grin and got in his Crown Victoria.

Coop placed the bag on the floor of the passenger side and watched as the dog's nose followed the scent of the soup. Chicken, in all forms, was Gus' favorite. He and Aunt Camille were to the point they had to spell the word or Gus would get too excited when they discussed having chicken.

He detoured to AB's house and parked. He sent her a text to let her know he was outside and had a care package for her. A few minutes later she came to the door, wrapped in a heavy blanket, coughing.

He handed her the bag. "Myrtle assures me this is a magic cure."

She gave him a weak smile and croaked out, "I could use a giant dose of magic."

Coop told her to call if she needed anything else. "Get some rest." Gus had his face pressed against the window, whining. "Gus misses you," he said.

They made their way to the office and started a fire and a pot of coffee. Without AB there, he decided to cheat and have real coffee. He'd need it to get through the day. Coop dug into AB's stack and found the files he had to finish. He gathered them and trudged to his office.

He put in several hours on the reports between answering the phone and checking emails. He went to staple the final report and discovered he was out of staples. He knew AB kept a stash in her drawer.

He opened the drawer and found the box along with a banded stack of letters addressed to him. The return address was scrawled with the name of his mother, in care of the county jail in Vermont.

He pulled them out and took the box of staples. He set the envelopes on the edge of his desk and focused on the task at hand. As he typed the reports, his eyes darted to the letters. They taunted him. He turned away, intent on finishing his work.

He opted to forage in the fridge for lunch and reheated some soup, wishing he had thought ahead to get an order of Myrtle's soup for himself. He ate at his desk as he worked. As much as he tried to concentrate on the tasks at hand, his thoughts drifted to the letters AB had kept from him.

He knew she was trying to protect him. "Does she think I can't handle more berating from my mom?" he asked Gus. The dog raised his ears but kept his head on the arm of the chair.

He finished the files and slipped the corporate reports into a mailing envelope after submitting them electronically. His cell phone played the music from *Perry Mason*.

"Hey, what's up, Ben?"

"I've got tickets to the Predators tomorrow night. Wanna join me?"

Coop's mood brightened. "That sounds terrific. How about dinner first, my treat?" They made plans to meet at one of their favorite barbeque restaurants downtown before the game. Coop glanced at the clock and realized he needed to get moving to get the mail to the post office.

He made his way through the office, turned out lights, shut off the copier and coffee maker, and turned down the heat. With Gus at his heels, he made his way to the alarm panel at the back door. He started to punch in the code when he remembered the packet of letters.

He hurried back and grabbed them and stuffed them in his jacket pocket. After dropping the mail, he stopped and picked up the pizza he had ordered for tonight. Aunt Camille was going to one of her club meetings, and he had told Mrs. Henderson not to worry about dinner.

He retrieved the pizza box, which Gus inspected with the intensity of a bomb dog and headed home for the weekend. He turned on the big screen television and put a few slices on a plate before grabbing a cold beer.

He sent a text to AB to check on her as he settled in for a night of mindless television and junk food. He polished off his last piece of pizza and stashed the rest in the fridge. Gus was already asleep on the couch next to him.

He flipped through the channels in search of an escape from reality. His phone beeped, and he scanned the return text from AB. She felt better and slept most of the day. She confirmed the superpower of the soup and thanked him again.

His fingers hovered over the keys, debating whether to ask her about the letters. He sent a quick text telling her he found the letters in her drawer and hadn't opened them.

His phone chirped again, and he smiled when he read it. *Was waiting until we're done with the case. Didn't figure there would be any good news in them and thought you have enough to deal with right now. Wait for me, please. I'll read them with you.*

It was impossible for him to stay mad at AB for over a minute. He replied back and promised to wait until she could be there, ending it with *Sunday supper, if you're up to it?*

Her response was pure AB. *"I'd have to be in the hospital to miss Sunday supper. I'll be there.*

Coop rested his head against the comfortable leather and smiled. He realized he didn't want to face the letters without her.

Chapter 13

The weekend plans for Coop consisted of only fun. No work, for a change. Coop spent a lazy Saturday morning visiting with Aunt Camille. Her club was planning an extravagant gala next month, and she was excited to share the details with Coop.

He listened to her describe the dinner and fundraiser she was helping to organize. He and Gus took a walk to the park. As he slipped his hand into his pocket, he felt the weight of the letters from his mother. He pushed them to the back of his mind and reached for a ball instead.

Gus romped through the grass and chased the ball, bringing it back to his master. The dog took delight in teasing Coop, moving his head each time Coop reached for the ball. After an hour of wrestling and laughing with Gus, any concern over the state of his relationship with his mother evaporated.

After completing a few minor chores around the house, he got ready for the evening with Ben. He found Aunt Camille in her sitting room with Gus plopped on the cushion beside her. She looked over the top of her reading glasses, "You look like an official team member in your gold and navy."

He put on his hat and said, "I'm off. You be a good boy for Aunt Camille," he said, patting Gus on the head.

"Oh, we've got big plans. He's going to help me select the

centerpieces and the menu for our gala. Aren't you, Gus?" She stroked his ear.

The dog's gentle brown eyes pleaded with Coop. "Sorry, big guy. You can't come tonight." The dog let out a sigh and placed his head against Camille's leg.

Coop made his way downtown and found a parking place. He knew he'd be fighting for a spot with almost twenty thousand other fans. He and Ben both parked in the courthouse garage.

Coop walked the few blocks to the restaurant and wiggled his way through the bar area, full of loud fans gearing up for the game. He found Ben at their table. They stuffed themselves on hefty servings of smoked brisket and pulled pork, along with plenty of sides and gallons of sweet tea.

As game time neared, the place became more crowded. They settled their bill and made their way through the crowded sidewalks to the Bridgestone Arena. Jen had given Ben the gift of Predator tickets to ten games. In essence, she had given Coop the same present, since she wasn't a diehard hockey fan and volunteered her seat for most of the games.

All of the entrances had huge lines. Ben had to check in with security, due to the fact he was armed. Ben never went anywhere without his weapon, and he was technically on call every minute of the day. He saw one of the security guys he knew and waved. Clyde had retired from the police department and worked part-time at the arena. "Hey, Chief, how are you?" He shook Coop's hand as they walked to the security office.

They bantered for a few minutes with some of the other officers while Clyde logged in both of Ben's weapons and his information on their form. "You're not carrying tonight, Coop?" he asked.

Coop put his hands up, "No, I'm clean tonight." Clyde put Coop through the metal detector and guided Ben around it as he escorted them to the VIP entrance into the arena.

"Enjoy the game," said Clyde, as he left them to find their seats.

They had a great view, seated in the first section next to the ice. They were several rows up but could see all the action. Despite only sixty minutes of total play time, they had been there for over two hours. The Predators were winning, and unless something catastrophic occurred, they would triumph over the Arizona Coyotes.

Over the loud cheers from the fans, Ben motioned to Coop and they started up the stairs to make their way out ahead of the thousands of hockey fanatics. Ben wasn't much for crowds, but his love of hockey trumped his aversion to large masses of screaming people, most of whom were full of beer.

They squirmed their way through the arena and outside, where the crisp day had turned downright frigid. The sidewalks were less populated, and they only heard the loud cheering when they walked by restaurants or bars where fans gathered to celebrate.

As they traversed the blocks to the courthouse, two young men darted out from a dark alley. One of them brandished a knife and said, "Give us your wallets."

Ben looked at Coop. Coop threw his hands up with a fast movement. "Don't be stupid," he said.

The pair were distracted by Coop's movements, and Ben pulled out his gun and said, "Police. Drop the knife and put your hands up."

The unarmed man took his eyes off Coop when he heard Ben, which gave Coop a moment to act. He rushed forward and slammed his shoulder into the young man, knocking him to the ground. Coop then flipped him over and sat on his back.

The tackle drew the attention of the knife-wielding man who turned to watch. Ben flashed forward and knocked the knife from the young man's hand and slammed him into the side of the building. "You picked the wrong guys tonight," he said, as he patted him down and handcuffed him.

He used his phone to call for assistance, and within minutes a patrol car pulled to the sidewalk, lights flashing. The officers handcuffed the man Coop had subdued. Another patrol car arrived and took custody of the suspect Ben had handcuffed. Ben recovered cell phones, credit cards, jewelry and a wad of cash from his would-be mugger and when the officers searched Coop's assailant, they found more of the same.

Ben eyed the alley and saw several dumpsters. "Search those dumpsters and the ground. Get some lights in there. I think they've probably dumped the wallets."

After retrieving his Jeep, Coop followed Ben to the precinct to fill out a statement. He didn't get home until almost midnight. Aunt Camille's light was out, and Gus was asleep near Coop's door, waiting for him.

The adrenaline that had carried him for the last few hours, during and after the scuffle with the two deadbeats, was beginning to wane. Gus followed him to his wing of the house and plopped onto his bed. Coop did the same a few minutes later.

* * *

Sunday morning Coop woke to the smell of coffee brewing. He had slept for eight straight hours. It was an unexpected gift. He found Gus with Aunt Camille in the kitchen. He was convinced the dog could cook if he had thumbs.

Aunt Camille had already eaten but fixed a plate for Coop. "Did y'all have fun last night?" she asked, placing his favorite oversized mug of coffee in front of him.

"Dinner was good, and the game was a lot of fun. We had great seats. The excitement came after the game."

As he ate, he entertained her with a blow-by-blow description of their encounter with the muggers. When he got to the part about the hoodlum brandishing a knife, Aunt Camille gasped. "Oh, my, Cooper. You boys could have been hurt."

"Not with Ben there. He's always packing at least two guns. The guy is as cool as a cucumber. It was a textbook takedown. We were a great team. Too bad it wasn't caught on video."

She shook her head and smiled. "Those hooligans messed with the wrong guys."

Their conversation turned to reliving some of Uncle John's most memorable stories. "Remember when he cleared four dozen outstanding warrants in one day?" asked Aunt Camille.

Coop grinned. "Yeah, he called them all to tell them they won a prize and had to claim it in person. That was priceless."

They lingered at the table and Coop watched his aunt's eyes sparkle when she spoke of her late husband. "Your uncle would be so proud of you, Coop."

He patted her hand and said, "That means the world to me. I only wish he was still by my side."

* * *

After a visit to the gym, Coop donned his "May your coffee be strong and your Mondays be short" t-shirt his brother had sent him for Christmas. When he arrived at the office, he found AB warming her back by the fire, a shrewd grin on her face.

Gus bounded over to her, waiting for a cuddle. Coop took off his jacket, and she said, "Nice shirt. Perfect for today."

He twirled like a model on a runway. "So, what has you looking so clever on this early Monday morning?"

"I think I found a link."

Coop's eyes flickered with interest. "Do tell."

"I've been combing through social media profiles looking for links between any of the people in our suspect pool and the scientists. I finally hit on something this morning. One of the visitors to Borlund the day of the murder, Scott Rayburn. The log says he's from the State of Tennessee. He's a compliance auditor and visited the administration area to conduct some sort of audit. Anyway, one of the janitors, Brett, is listed as a friend of Scott's. Not only that, but Scott also has a friend who shares the last name of one of our hate mailers, Mr. Benning.

She went on to explain how she hadn't found any direct connections between the hate mailers and anyone at Borlund but had started digging into their friends. She discovered a person named Cole Benning, who is a nephew of the hate mailer. "Cole is a social media friend of the auditor who visited the facility the morning of Neil's murder."

Coop squinted as he worked to follow the links. Coop was not a user of social media. He loathed the concept of it, but it had proven to be a treasure trove of information in many of his investigations.

"Okay, I think I've got it. So we need to bring in the auditor and find out what he can tell us and have a chat with Cole Benning to see how deep the river of hate for Borlund runs."

"I'll get in touch with them and set up appointments for you," she offered.

Coop found a photo of Scott Rayburn online and scanned the camera footage from Borlund until he located him. He watched him enter the building at 9:29 a.m. and saw him at the security desk.

He then saw him walk into the cafeteria. Coop searched the cameras for a view of the serving line and spotted Scott collecting a pastry and a cup of coffee. A few minutes later, he left the cafeteria and walked in the direction of the men's room. Coop picked him up again when he came out of the restroom and used the main stairs off the lobby.

He scanned the cameras and found Scott entering the administrative suite on the second floor. An hour and ten minutes later Scott emerged from the suite and again took the stairs. Four minutes later he was at the security desk checking out and then left the building at 11:07 a.m.

He sent Ben a text to keep him up to date on their findings and asked that his techs hone in on Scott Rayburn and get a good look at his shoes. AB appeared in the doorway and said, "You're set up with Scott at his office this afternoon. Brett starts his shift at Borlund at three this afternoon, so you can swing by there when you're done and surprise him."

His lips curved into a cunning smile. "I like how you think, AB." They spent the rest of the morning online, mining the social media profiles of Scott and Brett. They found nothing suspicious and no further links between anyone else affiliated with Borlund Sciences.

Coop left Gus with AB and drove north of the downtown area a few miles to a nondescript office building. The government ran out of room in the state-owned buildings years ago and shuffled some departments to leased offices. The Department of Labor took up several floors of the building.

Coop found Scott's office suite and was directed to a cubicle in the middle of the room. Coop introduced himself and explained he was working with the police and Mr. Hollund to investigate Neil Borden's death. Scott led Coop to a small conference room on the edge of the maze of workstations.

"I read about his death in the paper and was stunned to learn it's been deemed a homicide. How can I help?" asked Scott, offering Coop a chair. "I never met Mr. Borden or Mr. Hollund. My main point of contact there is Paula in payroll."

"I'm taking a look at people in the building the day of the murder. You visited that morning."

"Yes, I was doing a follow-up on the audit we conducted a couple of months ago."

"How did they do?" asked Coop.

"Huh? Oh, fine. No issues. They have a crackerjack staff."

"Take me through your visit to Borlund that day. Where did you go in the building? Who did you talk to while you were there?"

Scott sat back in his chair and frowned. "Let's see, I came here to the office first and would guess I got there around nine-thirty. I checked in with security and went upstairs to meet Paula. I talked to the guy at the security counter and the receptionist in the accounting suite, plus Paula. I think that's it."

"Did you visit the cafeteria or any other areas?"

His eyes widened. "Oh, yeah. I did stop at the cafeteria. They have great pastries. I got one and a coffee before I went upstairs."

"So, that's it. Security, cafeteria, upstairs to Paula, and then you were done?"

Scott nodded. "That's all I remember."

"Did you use the elevator? Restroom?"

"No elevator. I try to use the stairs." He patted his stomach. "I need to exercise when I can, especially if I eat those pastries." He laughed and then added, "Oh, I did use the men's room down the hall from the cafeteria."

Coop scribbled a note. "How do you know Brett Adams?"

"Brett? He's one of the parents on my kid's soccer team."

"Do you socialize with him much?"

Scott's forehead wrinkled. "No, not at all."

"Have you ever visited him at Borlund?"

Scott's eyes donned recognition. "Ah, I forgot he worked there. That's right. No, I never visited Brett at work."

"So your relationship with Brett is limited to your interactions at soccer games?"

"Right. Exactly. We run into each other there. Say hello and chat about the kids. The parents take turns bringing snacks for practice, stuff like that. Sometimes we give other kids rides. That's the extent of my relationship with Brett."

"So you're friends on social media because…" Coop left the sentence open.

"Oh, yeah. All the parents connect with each other since it's an easy way to keep informed and stay up to date on the team news. The coach has a page for the team. All the parents are on it."

Coop nodded. "Okay, as I said, we're looking into everyone."

"I guess you are," Scott said with a laugh. "If you ever want a job as an auditor, let me know. You obviously have an eye for details."

Coop chuckled and then asked, "You also have a social media connection to Cole Benning. How do you know him?"

"Cole and I play in a men's softball league. We won't start up again until May."

"Have you known him a long time?"

"A few years. We've played in the over forty league together on the same team. I don't know him very well, just through the team."

"Do you know his family? In particular, an uncle named Richard Benning?"

Scott shook his head. "I don't think so." He shrugged. "He may have come to one of our games. I couldn't be certain."

"Have you ever heard Cole talk about Borlund? Dr. Hollund or Mr. Borden?"

Scott's eyes registered confusion, and he shook his head. "No, never."

"Cole has never quizzed you about your work concerning Borlund?"

"No, sir. It's never come up at all." He frowned and said, "What's Cole got to do with your investigation?"

"Probably nothing. We're just being careful and examining anything we find."

He thanked Scott for his cooperation and left him sitting dumbfounded in the conference room. "I'm sure I don't have to remind you to keep this confidential," said Coop as he made for the door.

"Of course. Not a problem."

Coop steered the Jeep back toward his office and turned for Borlund. It was after three, so he knew Brett would be at work. He stopped in Bernie's office and told him he needed to meet with the janitor.

Bernie consulted a computer and scrolled through some cameras. "He's in the cafeteria. It's deserted this time of day. That should make a good meeting spot."

Coop concurred and made his way down the hall. He found Brett wiping down tables and chairs. "Hey, Brett, not sure if you remember me."

"Sure thing. How y'all doing?"

"Great, thanks. I have a couple more questions for you."

"Sure, have a seat." He motioned him to a clean table near the fireplace.

"We're looking at everyone in the building the day of Neil's murder. We noticed Scott Rayburn visited and we also learned you're connected to Scott via social media. Could you explain your relationship to Scott?"

"Sure, his kid plays soccer with mine."

"Has he ever approached you about your work here at Borlund or quizzed you about procedures?"

A look of bewilderment flashed across Brett's face. "No. He's never even mentioned Borlund. We aren't close friends, just associated because of the soccer stuff. All the parents are connected with a team page."

"Okay, just needed to check it out. Thanks for your time."

* * *

It was quitting time when Coop parked at the office. He found AB and Gus waiting for him. "I looked into Cole Benning. He works at Vanderbilt. He's in maintenance. I did some checking, and he's scheduled to work tomorrow. He starts at seven." She turned off her computer and gathered her things. "I figured you didn't want to give him time to concoct a story."

"I'll call Ben and see if he wants to join in on the interview." He sat on the hearth and Gus took up a position next to him, within easy reach for nuzzling. "I don't think there's anything to the connection." He summarized his conversations with Brett and Scott. "We'll see what Cole has to say about his uncle and the threats."

"I was hoping you'd learn something from one of them. I guess that means I should keep digging through all the profiles."

"Let's see where Cole leads us. Then we'll decide where to go. Thanks for all the hard work on this, AB."

She bent down and held the dog's face in her hands and looked eye to eye with Gus. "Good night, my favorite dog." She shoved Coop's shoulder on her way by them. "See ya tomorrow."

Gus looked at her with complete adoration before glancing at his master. Coop swore the dog winked. "She likes me, too," he said. Gus tilted his head and gave Coop a puzzled look.

Chapter 14

The next morning, Kate stopped by Coop's office bearing a box from AB's favorite French bakery. AB poured her a cup of coffee, and the threesome gathered around the kitchen table.

"We checked out the uncle, and we have no history of any contact with him. No traffic tickets. Nothing. His wife died a couple of years ago, just a few weeks before he wrote that letter," said Kate.

"Did you get a look at her file?" asked Coop.

Kate nodded as she swallowed a bite of her croissant. "Yeah. She was a diabetic. Had been for decades. She died of complications and was in the hospital at the time of her death. She'd been taking Borlund's drug for about a year."

"Let's go find Cole and see what he can tell us," said Coop, polishing off the rest of his coffee éclair. Gus didn't even try to follow Coop, he stationed himself next to the table, his eyes glued to the bakery box, waiting.

Kate drove and parked next to the maintenance office. They found the supervisor's office, and Kate introduced herself and Coop. She said, "We're looking for Cole Benning."

"I hope he's not in any trouble," said the older man.

"No, sir. Just hoping he can help us with an investigation we're working," said Kate. "It shouldn't take long."

The man consulted a matrix and said, "I'll give him a call and have him come back here. We've got a small conference room you can use."

Kate and Coop waited for about fifteen minutes before a man clad in coveralls came through the door. "I'm Cole Benning. Stuart said you wanted to see me?"

"Yes and we're sorry to interrupt your work. This should only take a few minutes," said Kate, introducing both of them.

Cole took a seat, and Kate explained they were in the middle of a homicide investigation concerning Neil Borden. "We're hoping you can help."

He frowned. "I don't know who Neil Borden is."

"Your uncle, Richard Benning, wrote this letter to Mr. Borden's company, Borlund Sciences." She slid a copy of the letter across the table.

Cole read through it, shaking his head. "Oh, yeah. Uncle Richard was positive the medication killed Aunt Doris. He was all fired up about it and wanted to sue the drug company."

"Does he still believe that now?" she asked.

"I don't know. I haven't heard my dad talk about it for a long time. From what I know the doctor tried to explain that it wasn't the medicine. We thought Uncle Richard was lashing out at the time. He had a hard time accepting her death."

Kate gave Coop a slight nod. "So, your uncle never asked you to help him get back at Borlund?" he asked.

Cole shook his head. "No. I don't see much of Uncle Richard. My parents moved to Florida last year. They come up once or twice a year, and that's when I see him. I've never been close."

Kate looked at her notes. "How do you know Scott Rayburn?"

"He's on my men's softball team."

"Do you socialize with him outside of the team?" she asked.

He looked confused. "No. I haven't seen him since the season ended last year. We'll start up again in May. How is he connected to this?"

"He isn't at this point. His job took him to Borlund Sciences the day of the murder, so we're checking out any of his connections that are tied to the victim. Since your uncle wrote a threatening letter and you knew him, we needed to get more information." Kate explained the need to conduct a thorough investigation.

"You've never visited Borlund Sciences?" asked Coop.

"No. Couldn't even tell you where it is," he said.

"Could we get your dad's contact information? I'd like to give him a call and ask about Richard," said Kate, handing him a pen and her notebook.

Cole wrote a few lines and slid it back to Kate. She looked it over and said, "Thanks for your time. We'll be in touch if we need anything else."

Cole nodded and shook their hands. "I really don't think Uncle Richard would do anything. He just needed someone to blame."

* * *

Kate called that afternoon after speaking with Cole's father. He had corroborated Cole's depiction of Richard's state of mind. She concluded the call by saying, "I don't see anything there. The old guy was upset and lashed out, but I don't think he had anything to do with Neil's death."

Coop moped in his office, staring at his whiteboard. All the promising leads had turned up nothing. His cell phone rang, and he saw his brother's name on the screen.

He smiled and answered, "Hey, Jack."

As Coop listened, concern replaced the happiness on his face. He nodded and scribbled on his notepad. "Okay, let me see what I can do. I'll call you as soon as I get things arranged."

He disconnected and trudged down the hall to AB's desk and dropped onto the couch. "Jack just called. Dad slipped when he was shoveling snow and hurt his knee. He's at the hospital with him now."

"Oh, no. Poor guy. Do you want me to book you a flight?"

"Check it out and see what's available. I'm going to run home and tell Aunt Camille and wait on more news from Jack. I'll keep you posted." He motioned to Gus, and they zipped out the door.

They found Camille in her sitting room. Coop explained the latest news from Nevada. As he was talking, Jack called again. He listened and asked several questions before disconnecting.

"Jack said the doctors want the swelling to go down before they do surgery. They said they could fix it arthroscopically, so that will make his recovery a bit easier. He's going to have to do a lot of physical therapy to strengthen the knee."

"Poor Charlie. Do you think we can convince him to come here to recuperate?"

Coop grimaced. "I don't know. He hates to travel. Jack and Molly both work though. They're not going to be able to stay with him during the day." He ran his fingers through his hair.

"I would like nothing more than to help Charlie. I know he'll be reluctant, but I have the means to charter a private plane to get him here. He wouldn't have to deal with all the rigmarole at the airport. It would be easy and quick. You could fly there and bring him back here." Her eyes flashed with delight as she contemplated the plan.

"That's very kind of you, Aunt Camille. I'm not sure I can convince him, but he's not going to want to be a burden to Jack. He's also not going to be cooperative about going to a rehab center. It might be his best option."

His phone pinged with a text from AB. She sent him the flight information for the next few days. He looked over the options and texted her back. "I'm going to fly out tomorrow and see if between the two of us we can convince him of your plan. Regardless, I want to be there when they do the surgery."

Camille petted Gus as she talked. "You remember Dolly from the garden club? Her granddaughter is a physical therapist. I'll give her a call and see if we can arrange for her to come to the house and do his therapy here. I'll pay if necessary, and we'll just tell Charlie it's covered by his insurance." She gave Coop a wink and nestled her rhinestone-encrusted reading glasses on her nose as she flipped through her address book.

Coop chuckled and bent down to kiss her cheek. "You missed your calling as a project manager."

"I love it when Charlie visits, and he hasn't been in here in such a long time. I hate that he's hurt, but I'm thrilled to think he'll be here." She put her finger in the address book. "I'll get the blue guest room all set for him. It's closest to your wing, so that will be the best spot for him. Mrs. Henderson and I will make sure he has good healthy meals to speed the healin' process."

"I'm sure it will take a few months of therapy. Maybe I can drive Dad home in March or April and stay for a visit. That might help convince him."

She bobbed her head and picked up the phone. "Good idea. I'll call Dolly now and see what I can arrange for therapy."

Coop went to his home office and called Jack. He explained Aunt Camille's plan. Jack thought it would be a tough sell, but agreed he couldn't work and take care of his dad.

"The doctor said they'll do surgery on Thursday. It shouldn't require an overnight stay. They were talking about sending him to a rehab facility. Dad didn't want anything to do with that idea." He sighed. "Sending him back there where he'd have someone to look after him is probably the best solution."

Coop gave him the flight information and his arrival time in Reno. Jack promised to be waiting for him when he arrived.

Coop retrieved a suitcase from a storage closet and packed his things. Gus, looking forlorn, knowing the big bag meant travel, stared at Coop. "I won't be gone long, buddy. AB and Aunt Camille will spoil you rotten. Don't you worry."

* * *

After a long, but uneventful travel day, Coop walked out of the airport and found his brother waiting at the curb. Jack greeted him with a hug and tossed his luggage in the trunk, before heading for the freeway. Coop sent AB a text to let her know he had landed. He felt guilty rushing away and leaving AB to deal with the investigation. She was more than capable and would contact him with any new developments, but he hated leaving her holding the bag.

The two brothers used the thirty-minute drive to discuss the latest updates about their dad's condition. Jack said, "Molly and I brought up the idea of him recovering with you and Camille." He related his dad's instant rejection of the suggestion.

"Molly and I have been hinting in front of him that it's going to be hard to manage his care, our jobs, and the kids. If you can reinforce how much free time Camille has and how much she wants him there, maybe it will help."

Coop agreed with Jack's idea of using guilt to guide their dad to Nashville. As they made their way out of the valley and headed up the hill into Carson City, he asked, "Do you think Dad's in good hands here?"

Jacked nodded. "Oh, yeah. We've got some of the best orthopedic guys around. Mostly because of skiers at Tahoe. He's got a top-notch guy, and the hospital is great. I got the doctor to schedule the surgery a little later in the day and that way Dad can stay the night and then hopefully we can get him on a plane with you Friday."

"Aunt Camille has one scheduled for us. She's been terrific."

Jack parked and led Coop to the modern building. They went upstairs to Charlie's room, and Coop marveled at the gorgeous views from the massive glass walls throughout the hospital.

Charlie was in bed watching television and eating pudding. Coop gripped his hand and said, "How ya doing, Dad?"

Charlie didn't hide his irritation at his circumstance. He was mad at himself for falling and irritated with everyone else because he was stuck in the hospital. "Jack told you we've got a plan to get you back to Nashville. Aunt Camille has a room ready and set up a physical therapist that will come right to the house to treat you. She's got everything arranged."

"I just don't know, Coop," said Charlie. "I'd sure rather be in my own house."

"I know, Dad. The problem is Jack and Molly work, plus they've got the kids. You'd have to go to a rehab place, and I know you don't want that."

Charlie shook his head in disgust. "I'm not going to one of those places. No way."

"Well, I guess that settles it. We'll fly back to Nashville on Friday. No hassle. Camille's got a plane coming for us. Then we'll get you settled and start your therapy Monday. The therapist will come by and meet you this weekend."

"Coop said he'd drive you back in a couple of months and stay for a visit when the kids have their break in April."

"Well driving back sounds good to me. I hate all the fuss with flying nowadays." Coop noticed his dad warming to the idea.

"Aunt Camille's working on menus with Mrs. Henderson.

Believe me, you'll get spoiled with their cooking." Coop smiled and handed his dad a glass of water. "Some of the best desserts you've ever tasted," added Coop.

He saw his dad acquiesce as he gave a hint of a smile. "I do love her pecan pie."

Coop breathed a silent sigh of relief. He didn't like trying to manipulate his dad but knew the best place for him was at Aunt Camille's. He'd never be without company or assistance. She'd be thrilled.

Charlie reached for Coop's hand. "Thanks for coming." He squeezed it. "You boys should go get some dinner. I'm going to get some rest for tomorrow. "

Jack approached his father. "It'll be easy, Dad. Doc says he's done thousands of them. He can do it with a spinal block, so you don't even have to be all the way out."

Charlie nodded and closed his eyes. "See you boys tomorrow."

Jack and Coop made their way out of the hospital and stopped for dinner at a place not far from Jack's house. "I need to check in with AB before it gets any later," Coop said, opting to have Jack order something for him while he stayed in the car and made his calls.

AB answered on the first ring. She asked about his dad and assured him she had let Aunt Camille know he had arrived in Reno. "Nothing new on the case. Still combing through social media connections and coming up empty."

"Did you talk to Ben?"

"Yeah, I let him know what was going on. He said not to worry. The DA is not anxious to press charges based on the circumstantial case, especially with all the strange things we've discovered about Neil. He's pressuring Ben to find more evidence."

"Easier said than done, I'm afraid." He told her he'd be flying back with his dad on Friday and would catch up with her over the weekend.

Next, he called Aunt Camille. He told her Charlie had surrendered and they would be flying back to Nashville on Friday. "I think the promise of your meals was the final straw."

With delight evident in her voice, she said, "What time will y'all be here?"

"Oh, it all depends on when they spring him from the hospital. I would think we couldn't get out of here until close to noon."

"Well, y'all have the number to call the service when you know the timetable. It should be less than five hours to get here. I'll send Mr. Henderson with the car to collect you at the airport. We'll have supper waitin'."

He promised to let her know when they were on their way.

"Give Charlie a big hug from me. Tell him he's made me happier than a pig in a mud hole on a hot summer day."

Coop contained a laugh. "I'll do that. Tell Gus I'll see him soon. See you Friday."

* * *

Charlie's surgery was a success. The surgeon's office had been in touch with an orthopedist from Vanderbilt who had been recommended to Coop by his doctor. Charlie was to follow-up with the new doctor next week and start his rehabilitation therapy as soon as possible.

Charlie was in better spirits Friday morning. Coop and Jack had stopped by the house and packed up Charlie's belongings. Jack promised to keep an eye on the place and take care of things while he was away.

They made it to the airport before noon and used a wheelchair to get Charlie onto the private jet. They were the only two passengers in the well-appointed cabin. A flight attendant offered them drinks and food.

As the plane cruised along, Charlie took a drink of his soda and said, "A guy could get used to this." The two chatted for a few minutes, but it was clear the exertion had exhausted Charlie. He soon fell asleep, and Coop put a soft blanket over him.

In between a few short naps, Coop thought about Chandler's case. He rehashed the ground they had covered and doodled on a notepad, searching for an epiphany in the squiggles and designs. Charlie slept the entire flight.

The plane landed at the small airport not far from Camille's house. The attendant helped get Charlie to the waiting vehicle, where Coop saw Mr. Henderson. "Mr. Cooper, how are you?" said the gentle man who had been a fixture at Aunt Camille's for as long as Coop could remember.

"Just fine. Thank you for coming to pick us up."

"Your aunt sent the SUV. Thought it would be easier for Mr. Charlie."

They helped Charlie get situated, and Coop loaded the luggage in the cargo area. Mr. Henderson chatted as he drove the short distance from John C. Tune Airport to Camille's estate.

Aunt Camille, Gus, and AB welcomed them at the door. The scent of roasting meat drifted through the air, and Coop's stomach rumbled. Mr. Henderson helped Charlie into the house. AB and Coop hauled in the pile of luggage and Gus trotted after Coop.

The dining table was set for dinner, and there was a new addition to the room. A fancy leather recliner with a remote control occupied one corner. Mr. Henderson and Coop helped Charlie into the chair, and Camille demonstrated the buttons on the remote, which adjusted the leg rest, back, and lifted the occupant out of the chair to make it easier to stand.

Charlie was fascinated with the technology. "Well, that's something. I've never seen anything quite like this." He settled into the soft leather, and Mrs. Henderson appeared with a tray which she put on another new contraption. It was a table on wheels like the hospital used to let patients eat in bed.

Charlie looked comfortable and content as he eyed the pot roast and mashed potatoes smothered in rich gravy. Camille bustled about the room and made sure Charlie was warm enough before she settled into her chair.

The table had been repositioned to allow Charlie's new chair to be part of the conversation circle. He talked nonstop about the plane and how easy the trip had been and how much he appreciated Camille's generosity.

"Don't give it a thought. John just loved you to bits, and I'm so excited to have you here. We'll have all sorts of fun."

AB and Coop discussed the case and recapped it for Charlie's benefit. Aunt Camille brought out a pecan pie for dessert. She handed a plate to Charlie, her smile beaming. "It's so excitin' when these two are here and have a case to solve." She handed plates to Coop and AB. "I just love helping y'all with your work. "She turned to face Charlie. "I helped them with their last case, you know. It was a doozy."

Coop and AB cleared the dishes while Camille regaled Charlie with an embellished version of her role in Coop's last case involving a murder. Charlie played right into her hand, asking her questions and gasping at the juicy parts. AB handed Coop a plate for the dishwasher and said, "It's wonderful to see her so happy again."

Coop listened to the laughter coming from the dining room and said, "Just like old times."

Chapter 15

Coop spent the weekend getting things organized for his dad and took him for a drive through the neighborhood, including the route to the office, to get him acclimated. Coop bypassed Aunt Camille's driveway and continued to the park. "Gus and I love to walk to the park when the weather is cooperative. Once you're more mobile, you can tag along."

The physical therapist, Annie, came to the house Saturday afternoon. She evaluated Charlie and scheduled his appointments for the next month. She would be there each weekday, and a home care nurse would check on him twice a week.

Mrs. Henderson and Aunt Camille fussed over Charlie and kept him amused and well-fed over the weekend. Coop had been uncertain if he would tolerate the constant interaction, but Charlie looked to be enjoying it. Coop took comfort seeing his dad relaxed and happy, which made it easier to leave him Monday morning.

AB was already at work when Coop and Gus arrived. He caught up on what he missed last week and signed the items AB had left on his desk. He handed her a file and turned when he heard the front door release.

A woman who looked to be in her forties greeted them with a weak smile. "You must be Mr. Harrington?"

"Yes, ma'am. Please call me Coop, and this is Annabelle.

Everyone calls her AB. How can we help you?"

"I'm Darla. Darla Fontaine. I'm a client at Bella's."

Coop frowned, and AB nodded her understanding and said, "At the salon?"

Darla bobbed her head. "That's right. The ladies suggested I come and see you. Your Aunt Camille is one of their favorite clients. They said you've helped out Daisy in the past and could probably help me."

"We'll do our best," said Coop, wondering what his aunt had gotten him into this time. He led Darla to his office and booted Gus off his chair and out the door. AB brought in a pot of tea and joined them at the conference table.

"I'm not sure where to begin," said Darla. "I'm embarrassed to be here."

"No need to be embarrassed. Why don't you tell us the problem you're hoping we can solve for you?"

She took a deep breath. "It's my son. He's missing. I need you to help me find him."

Coop picked up a pen and poised it over a notepad. "Let's start with some details. How old is your son?"

"He's twenty. The police said there's nothing they can do. He's an adult."

"I understand." He asked her for his name and a physical description along with prodding her to tell the story of her son's disappearance from the beginning. Darla explained her son, Tyler, had been attending Clark College but had quit at the semester break. He hadn't been heard from in a week. He left for work and never came home.

He worked at a part-time job at a grocery store and had moved back in with Darla when he quit school. Coop asked, "Did he seem depressed or unhappy?"

She shrugged, "He seemed a little lost. Like he wasn't sure what he was going to do."

Darla took out a folded piece of paper from her purse, and AB wrote down Tyler's financial information and social security number while Coop continued his questions. "Does he have relatives or friends he would go to?"

Darla shook her head. "I've contacted everyone I can think of. I've messaged Tyler online, texted him, called him hundreds of times. Nothing. No response. I found his phone in a drawer in his room. He never goes anywhere without it."

"What about his father?"

"He lives in Wyoming and hasn't seen Tyler for years. I did call him and told him he was missing, just in case he heard from him."

Coop made copies of Tyler's photos and took down all the information she provided plus the name of the police officer who had taken the report she filed. Darla asked about the cost and Coop said, "I'm hoping we can get a lead on your son quickly. "He gave her a number that was less than half of what he should have charged and saw the relief in her eyes. He explained he was giving her a discount and she could decide if she wanted to proceed further after their initial work.

She wrote out a check and handed it to him. "Thank you so much, Mr. Harrington. I appreciate you giving me a deal. I don't have much money, but Tyler…" she began to cry.

He stood and put a hand on her shoulder and guided her out of the chair. "Try not to worry. Sometimes young men need time alone. That could be all this is with Tyler."

AB followed Darla to the front area and promised to call the moment they had any news. She took Coop's notes and started the process of searching for the young man.

Coop put in a call to the police and talked to the officer. He knew what the officer would say, but wanted to make contact. Tyler was not a known drug user and had no mental health issues. He wasn't considered a threat to anyone and had no criminal history. The police couldn't do much since he wasn't a juvenile.

He let the officer know the mother had retained his services and the officer added that information to the report. Coop wanted the police to understand the mother was worried enough to pay for information concerning her son.

He joined AB at her desk as she was running Tyler through the system. "Looks like Tyler has another credit card. A new one, his mother didn't know about." She handed Coop a page from her printer.

"Looks like he's making his way across the country. Motels and gas stations."

"He's in Texas. Made a purchase today outside of Dallas." AB tapped more keys on her keyboard.

"He probably bought a burner phone at one of those convenience stores. No way to get in touch with him."

"We could wait for another motel charge and call them tonight. Ask for his room. Explain how worried his mother is. Maybe convince him to get in touch with her."

Coop nodded. "That's about the only thing we can do. Verify it is him and not someone using his card. Keep an eye on it and monitor it. "

"I've got an appointment after work, so I can't stay tonight," said AB.

"No problem. I can hang out until he stops for the night." Coop scratched Gus under his chin. "We'll let Aunt Camille know we'll be late."

While he waited for Tyler to stop for gas or a motel, he dug into the case files on Neil's murder. After reading through it, he put in a call to Chandler. "Hey, Chandler. How are you feeling?"

"A little better. It's just hard to get around. The bruising is fading, so that's good."

"I'm sorry I had to leave last week. AB said she explained about my dad."

"I understand. Not a problem. "

"Have you had any security problems or caught anything on camera?"

Chandler chuckled. "Only a few critters in the middle of the night. Gave me a heart attack when the alert woke me."

"That's good news. You don't need any more excitement. We're at a real standstill here. All the leads we followed amounted to nothing. Are you certain someone at the FDA or a competitor couldn't have been involved?"

"I don't see how. The FDA staff members were never alone with the drug. Our competitors have never been in the lab. Someone on the inside would have had to give them the drug."

"Or pay someone to dose you and take you out. Eliminate the competition. Without you Borlund would fold."

"If something happened to me, Neil could have secured another lead research scientist. CX-232 is already in the pipeline. My work on it is nearly done. My team could carry on with that without a problem."

"Give it some thought. If you were eliminated, which of your competitors would benefit?"

"I'll let you know, but off the top of my head, I can't imagine it."

* * *

After AB left, Coop and Gus monitored Tyler's credit card and minutes after seven o'clock he saw a charge appear from a motel in Albuquerque. Coop looked up the motel and put it in a call to the front desk of the modest motel chain.

Coop asked for a manager and explained he was a private investigator from Nashville working the case of a missing person. He provided Tyler's name and said, "We just saw the charge come through on his credit card. I'd like to verify the person is, in fact, Tyler and then have you connect me to his room. His mother is very concerned about him."

It took a few minutes to convince the manager, but Coop faxed a photo of Tyler, along with his driver's license. He waited on hold while the manager reviewed the documents. Several minutes later the manager came on the line and said, "The young man in the photo is the same person who checked in here alone. He stated only one person in the room. I'll put you through now."

Coop listened to the loud click of the transfer and then waited for Tyler to answer. After three rings he heard a tentative voice say, "Hello?"

"Tyler, my name is Coop Harrington. I'm calling on behalf of your mother. She's very concerned about you and hired me to try to find you. I'm a private investigator from Nashville."

"How, how did you know where I was?" asked Tyler.

"We tracked your new credit card. Looks like you're driving across the country. Are you doing okay, Tyler?"

"Yeah, yeah, I'm fine. I, uh, just needed to get away."

"Do you think you could call your mom? She's concerned and hasn't been able to get in touch with you. You left your phone behind."

Tyler sighed and said nothing for several seconds. Coop feared he would disconnect the call. "Tyler, I get it. I told your mom sometimes guys just need time away. She just wants to make sure you're okay. She was worried you might have been kidnapped."

"No, I'm okay. I'm thinking about going to see my dad. I'm not sure. I'm not sure what to do."

"Do you need money? Are you getting along okay?"

"I've got some money saved up and took some with me. I'm okay."

"How's your truck running? Have you encountered snow?"

"Yeah, I'm worried about that. I've been trying to figure out a route to avoid it."

"Maybe you could call your dad and let him know you're coming. He might know the best route or even meet you. You don't want to tackle mountain passes if you're not familiar with the area."

In a voice so low Coop had to strain to hear him, Tyler said, "Do you think he'd come?"

"I'm sure of it. I can make the call for you if you want?"

Coop waited for Tyler's response. "Yeah, I think that's a good idea."

"Give me your number, and I'll call your dad. I'm also going to let your mom know you're okay. She's going to want to hear from you."

Tyler recited a number. "I'm sorry. I'll call her."

"You go get something to eat, and I'll give your dad a call and give him your number. You can work out a plan with him. If you promise to call your mom, I'll hold off calling her and let you do it."

"Yes, sir. I'll call her as soon as we hang up here. Give me ten minutes."

Coop disconnected and called the number Darla had given him for her ex-husband in Wyoming. He reached Mr. Fontaine and explained he was working for Darla and had located Tyler. After sharing Tyler's phone number and location he disconnected and made his way around the office, shutting down things for the evening.

He looked at the clock and drummed his fingers on the desk. His promise to Tyler conflicted with his commitment to his client. He gave Tyler all the time he dared. He dialed Darla's number, and she answered on the first ring. "Darla, it's Coop Harrington. I'm just calling—"

Her excited voice interrupted him. "Oh, Mr. Harrington. Thank you. Thank you. I just can't thank you enough. Tyler just called and told me he's going to see his dad. He wants to stay there for a bit and figure things out." He heard a stifled sob. "I'm so relieved to know he's alive. I'm going to try to give him some space. As long as I know he's safe, that's all that matters."

"I'm glad we found him. I wish you both the best." He explained he talked to Mr. Fontaine and he agreed to get in touch with Tyler and meet him on the road. He thought it best to guide him to Wyoming.

She extended her heartfelt gratitude again and again. Coop let her ramble on and wished her a good evening. He made his way to the back door with Gus close behind. "Well, old buddy, that was a happy ending to the day." Coop set the alarm and Gus watched, thumping his tail.

* * *

Darla visited the office the next afternoon, toting a huge basket of homemade cookies and brownies and other calorie-laden snacks. From his window, Coop saw her park and made himself scare behind closed doors. AB visited with her and accepted the thank you gift with grace and sincere appreciation.

"Tell Mr. Harrington I'm forever in his debt. His aunt always talks about what a great detective he is and now I'm a believer." She waved as she left and again when she got to her car.

Coop waited for her to drive away before he opened his office door. He found AB in the kitchen inspecting the treats. She had a giant cookie in her hand and took a bite. "This is yummy."

He eyed the gift and nicked a cookie. "We've got to finish those security assessments." Many of their clients hired Harrington and Associates to assess their security procedures. Madison and Ross took delight in going undercover and working to breach security at several large firms in the area.

"Right. One of them should result in more work for us. Madison and Ross were able to penetrate several areas in the company. They'll want recommendations for improvements. The other one wasn't bad."

"Okay, let's try and wrap those up this week. I talked to Chandler, and there's nothing new on his end. The case is stalled. I don't think the DA is going to make a move, so we've got a little breathing space. We've got to find someone with a motive."

"By the way, Aunt Camille wanted me to invite you to supper tonight. Mrs. Henderson is making fried chicken. Coconut cream cake and chocolate cream pie for dessert."

"Three things I can't resist. I'll be there, thanks." She took a file from her desk and handed it to Coop. "I'll work on the summary, and you can do the recommendations." The reports consumed the afternoon, and soon it was time to close the office.

AB grabbed a small stack of envelopes from her desk. "The latest from your mother," she said, handing them to Coop.

"Gee, thanks. I guess I should read these sometime soon." He motioned to Gus, and they followed AB to Camille's house. They entered to laughter and the kitchen noises of meal preparations.

Coop tossed the letters on the buffet and made his way to the kitchen. His dad was propped in a chair, watching Camille and Mrs. Henderson. Aunt Camille was the first to spot Coop and AB. "Oh, good y'all are off on time tonight. How are you, AB? So glad you could join us."

"I couldn't resist the menu," she said, hugging Camille. "Can we help?"

"We're almost done here. How about you and Coop get Charlie settled into his chair in the dining room?"

Coop moved to his dad and helped him up, and AB cleared the way for them to the dining room. "How was your therapy, Dad?" He handed Charlie the remote control for the chair.

"Good. Hurts a little. Annie tells me that's good." He laughed and added, "She's a firecracker. Missed her calling as a drill sergeant."

Coop smiled and wheeled the table in front of his dad. "That's good. No slacking."

Camille and Mrs. Henderson carried platters and serving bowls to the table and AB poured sweet tea for the group. Mrs. Henderson wished everyone a pleasant evening and excused herself.

Camille fixed Charlie a plate and set it in front of him before passing things around the table. Coop had just taken his first bite of mashed potatoes when she gasped, "Oh, I was at Bella's today. You are the talk of the shop, Coop. Darla told them all about how you found her son. She thinks you're quite the superhero."

"Aww, it wasn't that tough of a task. I'm just glad the kid's okay."

"She even asked if you were single," she gave Coop a not so subtle wink.

He rolled his eyes. "Oh, boy. Just what I don't need. Tell her I'm taken."

"She thought you and AB were an item." Camille looked across the table at both of them. "I didn't correct her." She smiled and turned to Charlie. "Do you need another biscuit?"

Coop shook his head and raised his brows at AB. She shrugged and smiled. Camille continued chatting throughout the meal. Coop and AB offered to clear the table while Camille arranged a dessert tray.

None of them could decide between the two desserts, so they

took small slivers of each. As Coop slid his fork into the velvety chocolate pie, she said, "I told Charlie we have to go to the community center. They've got that fancy indoor track for exercise."

Charlie gave a nod. "Camille's trying to coerce me into joining a card playing group down there."

"All my friends are women. I was trying to think of something Charlie could do when I have my club meetin' and the like. They've got afternoon card games and bingo, plus a few other activities. It's a lovely building. Remember we went to the dedication, Coop?"

He finished off the pie and nodded. "Yeah, it's nice." Camille would be the only person who could persuade Charlie to go to a community center. Jack had tried to get him involved in something similar back home and had struck out.

"We're going to take a trip to the stables and visit the horses this week. That will be a pleasant outin'. Just need to make sure we have good weather." She turned to Charlie. "Do you need more dessert?"

He patted his stomach. "I couldn't eat another bite. It was delicious. I'll have leftovers tomorrow."

Camille beamed and puttered to the kitchen. "Oh, Coop, I meant to tell you. I found these letters on the floor by the coat closet. I think they fell out of your jacket."

She returned and put the stack of letters he had been avoiding in the palm of his hand.

"I brought home the others tonight. I guess we may as well read them."

Charlie's brow furrowed. "What letters are you talking about?"

Camille bit her lip and Coop muttered. "They're from Mom. She's in jail."

Chapter 17

Charlie's eyes widened. "Jail? Oh boy."

AB and Camille busied themselves to give Coop a bit of privacy with his dad. They promised to return with hot drinks and disappeared into the kitchen to clean up the dishes.

Coop took a deep breath. "You know Jack and I never talk about Mom with you. We used to, but we always saw how much it hurt you to hear about her escapades."

"I'm a big boy, son. I can handle it."

"Let's just say over the years, I've had to get involved and help her out of several situations. It was easier to plunk out some cash than to deal with her in my life. So, I've been the one she's called for help. Before Christmas, she showed up here."

"Here, at your aunt's house?" Coop saw the vein on the side of his father's forehead. It was a telltale sign of irritation. If it began to throb, experience dictated all bets were off.

"At my office and here. She was hinting that she wanted to spend Christmas with us. She was on her way to Vermont to visit a friend. I paid for a hotel and plane ticket and sent her to Vermont early."

"She called me a couple of weeks ago from a jail in Vermont." Coop related the story of her arrest and subsequent outburst in court and the resulting sentence. He retrieved the envelopes and placed them on the table. "She's been sending me letters."

Coop fiddled with his napkin. "More like hate mail. AB read a few of them and was keeping them from me. Didn't want me to get upset."

Charlie cleared his throat. "You'd probably be better off just tossing those in the fire and burning them. They'll be of no use to you."

Coop grinned. "Wise advice. You would think by now I would know better. Maybe it's the investigator in me. I keep trying to figure her out."

"I've given up on that front. Long ago. I finally realized she was an unhappy person and there was nothing I could do or say to make her happy." Charlie shifted in his chair and gave the wheeled table a shove. "It was years after she left that I understood that."

Camille and AB returned with a tray of tea and decaf coffee. "Here we are," said Camille. She made sure Charlie had a cup within easy reach and settled into her chair.

Coop shoved the stack of letters to AB. "Go ahead. Start on them."

AB clutched her chest. "Me? You want me to read them all?"

Charlie eyed the pile. "Apparently she's become quite the writer. She must mail one a day."

"Summarize them. We don't need to hear every word," said Coop.

AB took the pile and opened the first letter that was still sealed. She scanned the contents and Coop watched her eyes. "It's more of the same rambling, Coop." She sighed and said, "She blames you and her lawyer. She hates the food and can't believe they don't allow smoking. She's been buying snacks at the jail commissary and surviving on junk food. She has to buy coffee and decent shampoo."

She picked up another envelope. "Can't believe you're not bailing her out. She knows you have plenty of money and just won't help her. She's the only woman in the section for female prisoners." AB shook her head. "Because everyone else cares about their mothers."

She moved to the next one. "She had a visit from Ms. Flint."

"That's the lawyer I paid for her court appearances," added Coop.

"Ms. Flint asked Marlene if she knew how she was able to shop at the commissary in jail. She explained Coop had provided funds for Ms. Flint to deposit each week so Marlene would have access to items she wanted." AB's eyes left the page and found Coop's. "Your mom never gave it a thought. She says it's the least you could do for her."

Aunt Camille stirred her tea. "Well, y'all, I can't believe Marlene." She patted Coop's hand. "Don't let her hateful words bother you, dear."

AB opened the next letter. "She's complaining about not smoking again. Said they take her outside twice a day and she's having nicotine withdrawals. The jail has a tiny library with books she's afraid to touch for fear of what's on them. She used some of her money to buy two new paperbacks. She only gets to watch television one hour a day, but if she improves her behavior, they will bump it up to two hours a day."

Coop grinned. "Any bets on that one?"

His dad shook his head. "I think it's safe to say she'll be keeping her one hour a day program."

AB continued through the stack. Marlene lashed out at Coop and everyone concerned with the case. She was reminded she had to complete her community service upon her release and that started a new tirade against the system. They were also hounding Marlene to write her letter of apology. She wanted Coop to understand she had to buy the stationery and stamps to send him her letters.

AB summarized the criticism and lambasting Marlene dished out in each of her letters. She stumbled over words and phrases designed to excoriate Coop. AB stuffed the last letter back in its envelope. "I'm sorry, Coop. She's horrid. I wish you would have never found these in my desk."

Charlie said, "She's a real piece of work. I'm sorry, son. Listening to her nonsense is awful. Your mother's power over me dissolved years ago. It took a long time, but I'm past the point where what she says or thinks bothers me. I hope you can do the same."

"It's a shame Marlene hasn't done more with her life," said Camille. "Here words are pure rubbish. I had hoped she would come to her senses."

AB let out a long breath and stacked up the letters. "This is a lesson in futility. It's obvious your mother knows nothing about you. You're kind and always willing to help others. Your integrity and work ethic are respected throughout this community. It's too bad she's never taken the time to be in your life. She'd know what a great person you are."

She stood and stomped to the coat closet and shouted. "I can't read any more of her bull...baloney. If she comes around here again, I'll jerk a knot in her tail." She slipped her arms into her jacket as she came back into the dining room.

In her typical soft and polite voice, she added, "Thanks for dinner, Camille. Glad to see you doing well, Charlie. I'll see you at the office tomorrow, Coop." She gave Gus a quick nuzzle and was out the door.

Coop sprinted to the door chasing after her, Gus following. Charlie turned to Camille and said, "Atta girl."

Chapter 18

The evening reading did little to help Coop sleep. After spending almost half an hour standing on the cold concrete in his socks talking to AB, he lingered in front of the fire. His feet were so cold they burned as the warmth from the fire worked to thaw them.

Charlie and Camille had disappeared by the time he and Gus came back inside the house. He took a peek in his dad's room and saw him nestled in bed. He spent an hour staring at the flames, listening to the soft snores of Gus, and wrestling with thoughts of his mother.

He didn't want her words to have an impact. He knew she was angry and blaming him instead of herself. The logical part of his brain reiterated the facts. But there was a tiny part of him, the hint of a young boy still there that felt beaten.

He didn't allow himself to eat at night when he couldn't sleep. He had enough trouble maintaining his weight without the added calories but made an exception tonight. He scouted out the chocolate cream pie and cut a slab.

As he tasted the velvety chocolate and sweet whipped cream, it reminded him of the love surrounding him. He took in the home Uncle John and Aunt Camille had made. The home that had healed his wounds as a young college kid and shaped him into the man he had become. His dad, who in his quiet way, had let Coop go and make his own life. He was a man who had suffered his share of heartaches at the hand of the woman who should have been Coop's fiercest protector and fan.

It was well after midnight when Coop woke Gus from his spot by the fire and ushered him to the bedroom. By the time Coop climbed into bed, Gus was sound asleep again. He rested his head on the pillow while thoughts of AB churned in his mind. She had been ready to drive to Vermont and pay his mother a visit. He didn't think he'd ever find someone as loyal as Aunt Camille, but AB was the real deal. She'd never let him down and always had his back. A more faithful friend he'd never find.

* * *

The next morning, AB was at her desk when Coop and Gus arrived. She apologized for her outburst last night and then focused her attention on the reports they had to finish.

By noon, things were back to normal. The letters were forgotten. Coop picked up sandwiches for lunch, and they pounded through the afternoon. A couple of hours before closing time they heard a voice at the back door. "Yoo-hoo," said Aunt Camille. She asked Coop to help Charlie from the car and up the steps to the office.

Coop guided his dad to the ramp he had installed a couple of years ago. It was slow going, but Charlie did most of the work on his own. Coop helped him to a chair in the reception area.

"Whew, that was a workout," said Charlie, accepting a cup of tea from AB.

"What brings you two by?" asked Coop.

"We went to the community center today. We did two laps on the track and ate lunch there."

"It wasn't half bad," said Charlie. "Nothing like your meals, Camille, but not bad."

"Charlie met a few of the regulars and played some cards. My friend, Dixie, volunteers there. She was working today. She helped Charlie get acquainted."

"That sounds good. Did you like it there, Dad?"

"Yeah, it wasn't like the old folks place back home. They even have a woodworking shop. When I can get around better, I'm going to use it."

"They've got loads of activities. Arts and crafts, computers, photography, cards and games, a small library branch, a lovely coffee bar, plus a cafeteria. It's wonderful. I haven't been since the dedication."

AB offered one of the homemade treats Darla had baked them. "That sounds like fun."

"Well, there's also somethin' amiss down there. Dixie was telling me they've got more and more people comin' in. They accept donations, charge for some materials for the classes, and collect a small amount for lunch. She said there's somethin' wrong with the money. She has to count out the donations and the cash box before she leaves each day and said it's been growin' since the place opened. But, the woman in charge of the place keeps sayin' they don't have enough money and might have to cut their programs."

"Don't they get some funding from the county or city?" asked Coop.

Camille nodded and took a bite of her cookie. "These are yummy. That Darla is quite the baker. Yes, they get a certain amount of tax revenue, and they have grants and rely on donations."

Charlie finished his second cookie. "Dixie thinks somebody's pilfering funds. She said there's no reason they should have any financial trouble. The donations have gone way up. According to her, there's something fishy going on."

Coop held up his hands. "I can't get involved in this right now.

AB and I have a ton of work to get out this week, and we're still working on Chandler's case."

Camille smiled, and her eyes revealed her enthusiasm. "You don't need to get involved. Charlie and I are going to stake out the place and see if we can figure out what's goin' on."

AB hid a grin behind her cup. Coop forced himself to stifle a laugh. "What do you mean stake it out?"

"Oh, just spend time there and poke about to see what we can learn. I thought I'd sign up to volunteer like Dixie. Charlie can do some activities and play cards and see what he can overhear."

Charlie smiled at Coop with a glimmer in his eye. "I told your aunt I don't mind helping her plus I like their exercise track."

"Not to mention, your dad turned several heads at the place. The place is overrun with widows." Camille winked at Charlie.

He shook his head and chuckled. "As I've heard you say Camille, I need that Iike a submarine needs a screen door."

Camille flicked her hand at him and said, "Wouldn't it be grand if Charlie met someone and moved out here with y'all?"

"I'd like nothing more than to have Dad closer," said Coop. "I'm staying out of the matchmaking business." Coop noticed the tired look in his dad's eyes. "You look worn out. Time you get back home and rest." He stood and helped him out of the chair.

"Oh, my, yes. We've been out all day. After Charlie's therapy, we headed down there and haven't stopped since. We'll get home and get him a nap before supper." AB held her jacket, and she slipped into it. "Speaking of supper, come join us on Friday. We should have something to report by then, and you can help us figure it out, AB."

AB promised to be there and waved as Camille got behind the wheel and Coop settled Charlie into the passenger seat. He came up the steps, shaking his head in amusement.

She smiled at him. "That could be us in a few decades. Relegated to investigating shenanigans at the community center."

"Let's hope we're retired and sipping drinks on a beach somewhere by then."

* * *

In between typing up his security recommendations and signing checks, Coop checked in on Chandler. He hated telling him he still had nothing. No breakthroughs, no epiphanies. The case was getting colder with each passing day.

Chandler took the news well. He had adapted to his homebound status and was binge watching several series he had never heard of, much less seen. Coop stopped by with coffee or lunch a couple of times a week and promised to see Chandler again over the weekend. He left him with a couple of mystery books featuring a detective Coop thought Chandler would enjoy.

Despite the chill, Coop and Gus were able to get in a couple of walks to the park in the afternoon. Coop could only take so many hours of the tedious work on the security assessments, and much to the dog's delight ducked out early.

The dreary days of winter matched his mood. He had always hated January. Once the holidays were over, the gloom of the season commenced. The park was still a picturesque escape, despite the bare trees. It was the perfect quiet spot for a brief hiatus from work and all things real.

Gus romped while Coop contemplated. The case. His mother. Life in general. The bright spot in his otherwise dull existence was his dad. He hadn't realized how much he missed him. Having him around was comforting. Not to mention how much he had brightened Aunt Camille's life. It was going to be difficult for Coop to let him go after having him around for a few months.

Gus chased the ball for Coop when his nose didn't lead him to investigate ordinary shrubs or rocks. They watched an old man walking a small curly dog. The dog wore a yellow rain slicker and four tiny yellow boots. Gus titled his head at the pair and then turned to face Coop. "I don't have the answer for you buddy. Just be glad I don't buy you funny clothes."

* * *

Friday morning at breakfast Coop quizzed Ben about any developments in Chandler's case. "We've been busy with some new cases, so it's taken a backseat at the moment. Not to mention a bunch of the techs have been out with the flu. It's going through there like wildfire."

Coop backed away from the table. "I don't need any germs. I hate being sick."

Myrtle approached their table with a pot of fresh coffee. "I see your daddy's in town, Coop. He stopped by with Camille the other day. I haven't seen him in years."

"Yeah, he's recuperating with us for a few months."

She nodded. "He told me about his knee surgery. He was a bit gimpy, but in good spirits."

"Aunt Camille is keeping him busy and making sure he's well fed. He's enjoying all the attention."

"I hope y'all stop in on the weekends while he's here." She turned at the sound of the bell from the kitchen. "I better get. I've been busier than a moth in a mitten. I'll have AB's order out in a jiffy."

"Dad's turning the heads of septuagenarians throughout Nashville." Coop laughed and took a long slug of coffee.

"Jen wants to have y'all over for dinner while your dad's in town. When he's feeling up to it."

"He'll like that. He's making progress already between his

therapy and walking the track at the community center. Aunt Camille's roped him into helping her with one of her investigations." Coop used air quotes and entertained Ben with a condensed version of Camille's latest escapade.

They were both laughing when Myrtle returned with a box and their check. "It's nice to see you boys havin' fun. Y'all are usually all wrapped up in some crime."

Ben picked up the tab and waved to Coop as he and Gus headed to the office. AB took a break and ate her pecan pancakes while Coop reviewed their final reports. He was due to drop off the finished products after lunch.

They tweaked a few things, and then AB printed them and put them in fancy Harrington and Associates folders. She gave Coop's shirt the stink eye, and he acquiesced and put on a company button down over his "Bureaucrats delight in making the possible impossible" t-shirt.

"I'll leave Gus with you and if I'm not back when it's time to close, can you bring him to dinner with you?"

"Sure thing. We'll be fine." Gus, resting at AB's feet, gave Coop a look that said "Neener neener" with his tongue sticking out.

"Sometimes I think that dog is human," he said, gathering his satchel and hollering out a farewell.

* * *

Coop's visits to the two firms were successful. He secured a contract to implement his recommendations and a referral from the other client. After concluding his business meetings, he stopped by a smoothie place and drove to Chandler's house.

Chandler greeted him at the door, dressed in sweats. Coop handed him a smoothie. "Looks like you're making some progress. You've graduated from pajamas to sweatpants."

Chandler smiled and motioned him into the living room. "Yeah, it's been a good day. I've mastered putting on my pants with one hand."

"I think this time off has done you some good. You're less... serious."

"You think so? I haven't taken time off in years. It's been an adjustment, but the way our work is structured to safeguard our research, there isn't much I can do here at home. I hate to admit it, but I've almost enjoyed my time at home. I usually just sleep here and haven't ever spent time living in the place. I even used the computer to video chat with my family."

"How are they handling it?"

"They're concerned, but I've downplayed the whole thing. I don't want them to worry about me."

They talked about the case, commiserating over the lack of progress. Chandler asked about Coop's dad and extended an invitation to bring him by the next time Coop visited. "We could compare injuries," he said with a laugh.

Coop took out Chandler's garbage and did a few chores around the house that Chandler couldn't do with an injured hand. He made sure he had groceries and entertained him with Camille's theory about the scandal at the community center.

"Is that the Heritage Center in Belle Meade?"

Coop nodded. "You know it?"

"I've donated a ton of money to that place. I like the model of having a lot of activities for seniors and incorporating other age groups, so it doesn't become a dowdy senior center."

"I can assure you, if my aunt's on the case, she'll get to the bottom of it."

"Keep me posted. I'm happy to intervene. I have some pull with the board."

Coop finished his smoothie and inquired about Chandler's dinner plans. When he learned Chandler intended to order something delivered, he invited him to Aunt Camille's.

"Oh, I wouldn't feel right infringing on your family time. Heck, I'm a murder suspect. She may not want me in her house."

"Don't be silly. Come on and get ready. Think you can handle the Jeep?"

Chandler smiled and nodded his head. He moved as fast as he could manage to the master suite, and Coop helped him button a shirt and put on real pants. While Chandler finished getting ready, Coop called Aunt Camille to warn her about another guest.

Coop helped Chandler into a jacket and down the steps to the Jeep. When they arrived, AB greeted them at the front door. Chandler smiled and said, "Annabelle, nice to see you again." Coop excused himself to wash his hands and help Camille with her last minute preparations.

"Come on in. It's almost ready." AB helped Chandler out of his coat and guided him to the dining room, where Charlie was already seated in his fancy chair. AB introduced the two of them.

Coop carted platters and bowls to the table, and Camille followed behind with a basket of warm biscuits. She greeted Chandler and said, "I'm so pleased y'all could join us tonight. I've been followin' your case."

"I appreciate the invitation, ma'am. You have a lovely home, and I haven't had a home-cooked meal in years."

"It's Camille, and we'll remedy that right quick. Have a seat," she pointed to the chair closest to Charlie. They took their seats and passed pot roast, mushroom grits, potatoes, and roasted veggies around the table. As was her new habit, Camille fixed Charlie's plate for him.

AB helped Chandler when he struggled to serve himself. "Sorry,

I'm able to eat with my left hand, but serving is another matter." He took his first bite and said, "Miss Camille, this is the best pot roast I've ever tasted."

Her rosy cheeks glowed with joy. "I can't take all the credit. I have a wonderful cook and housekeeper who makes most of our meals. I'm happy you like it."

"Don't let her fool ya. She's an excellent cook. Her Sunday suppers are legendary," said AB.

Coop heaped a spoonful of veggies onto his plate. "I found out Chandler's one of the principal donors to the Heritage Center. I told him you suspected some wrongdoing."

Camille looked at Charlie and grinned. "We spent a lot of time there this week. I volunteered, like Dixie, and Charlie took some classes and played cards each day."

She explained the procedures volunteers followed. Patrons are issued cards, and their visits and use of the amenities are tracked by scanning the cards. The center published quarterly financial reports, and they were in binders in the library for public consumption. While Camille volunteered, she helped herself to the reports and took photos of the pertinent details with her cell phone.

"Charlie and I have been reviewing the reports and Dixie's right. The usage has been on the rise. The donations have been increasing. There's no reason they should be having financial trouble."

Charlie asked for another biscuit. "From what the guys say, the lady who runs the place is concerned they're going to have to cut programs and hours to keep from shutting down."

"I'm going to make a call to a couple of the board members. It's one of those advisory boards, so they don't handle the day to day operations. Seems like something has to be amiss if the revenue is there."

AB passed the pot roast and added, "It means the expense side needs a thorough audit."

Coop and AB discussed some of the cases they had been involved in and the financial irregularities they had uncovered. Camille nodded and said, "If there's somethin' fishy goin' on, it's got to be an inside job."

The diners agreed with her. "Who has access to the money?" asked Coop.

"The volunteers, the bookkeeper in the office, I would imagine the lady in charge, Ms. Stein."

"In our experience, either somebody is siphoning off some of the cash from the daily receipts, or there's something more sophisticated going on with the accounting end of the operation. Like AB said, if the income matches the cash sheets from the volunteers, it's on the expense side."

Chandler promised to make a call and get in touch with Aunt Camille on Monday. "I don't have much else to do. This will give me a new project." He smiled and asked for another helping.

* * *

Late Monday afternoon, Coop heard a horn honk in the back parking lot. Gus beat him to the door, tail in a frenzy of wagging. Coop saw Camille's sedan. She was out of the car opening the passenger door for Charlie. Coop did a double-take when he saw Chandler sitting in the back of her car.

He charged outside to help make sure his dad was steady on his feet and then helped Chandler. "We've got excitin' news and progress on our case," said Aunt Camille, as she popped the trunk and hefted out reams of computer printouts. Coop grabbed the bulk of them, and the foursome made their way into the office.

They gathered in the reception area, and AB readied a pot of tea, along with some of the leftover treats from their gift basket. Aunt Camille took a cup of tea and said, "Chandler has been a huge boon to the investigation y'all."

He smiled and thanked AB for the tea. "I just made a couple of calls. Got the ball rolling."

"Oh, it's rollin' along. Those board members made a surprise visit and took copies of all the transactions. Chandler got us our own copies. We volunteered to help go through them."

"Did we?" asked Coop, his brows arched.

"And Chandler dispatched two of his top-notch staffers from Borlund to go through the processes in the bookkeeping office and look at their software system."

"I'm no accounting wizard, so thought that would be the quickest way to get a good readout on the situation. The board was happy for the free help."

"And the office down at the center is all a flutter. I volunteered today and when the board members showed up the office went into a tizzy," Camille said with a wry smile.

Coop and AB leafed through some of the papers from Camille's trunk. "From the looks of these printouts they pay most of their bills electronically," said AB.

Coop nodded as he ran his finger down the list of transactions. "Are you thinking what I think you're thinking?"

With a knowing nod, AB said, "Chandler, ask your people who are at the office to check the vendor account numbers for electronic payments. We've run across a few schemes before that could be employed here." She explained that people working in the accounting offices had changed the account numbers for vendors or even just one vendor and diverted funds to their own accounts rather than pay the bills.

She continued to describe the methods used by embezzlers. "We've also seen them add fictitious vendors to the list. When we dug into them, it turns out they were linked to their own bank accounts."

"That's some sneaky stuff," said Charlie. "I don't understand the electronic craze nowadays."

"There are methods companies employ to make sure this kind of fraud doesn't happen." AB turned to Chandler, "You said the board doesn't get involved in the daily operations and with a small staff and limited oversight, it's the perfect environment for corrupt employees."

He finished his tea and returned the cup to the table. "I have a feeling there's going to be a change in that regard. They're going to have to take a more active role in the operations and put in more stringent safeguards. I'll call my staff now and tell them about the vendor angle." He pulled out his phone and punched some buttons.

Camille reached for another cookie. "It's disgustin' that people would steal from a program like that. Most of the patrons are seniors. Some of them lack the means to prepare or purchase meals, so they go there for lunch. It burns my biscuits."

The four waited and listened as Chandler made the call. He disconnected and said, "They've made a copy of the database, and the board members sent the office staff home until further notice. She said the vendor issue is on their list of things to investigate."

They finished their impromptu afternoon tea while speculating on what would happen if fraud was uncovered at the center. "They're going to take the database and records back to Borlund. She thought they would have some preliminary results tomorrow. They'll check the vendors first."

"The substitution of account numbers is one of the easier ways for crooks to embezzle without drawing much attention. It looks like things are normal, but it comes back to haunt them when actual bills are behind and aren't being paid. Many times they've moved on from the job by then and just took what they could get," said AB.

Coop stood and said, "Well, let's call it a day. Sounds like we'll know more tomorrow."

Camille insisted they gather for supper at her house tomorrow night and get the latest updates from Chandler's staff and his connections with the board members. "In the meantime, we'll look at these reports. I'm scheduled to volunteer again tomorrow, so I might learn somethin' then."

Chapter 19

Tuesday Coop and AB got caught up on their other casework. Coop had client meetings with two of his divorce cases, where suspected adultery was involved. He had to share damaging evidence implicating their spouses in affairs. He loathed spousal infidelity issues and was working hard to get more corporate work in an effort to abandon nasty divorce proceedings.

After his stressful meetings, he plopped onto the couch closest to AB's desk. "So, I think we should take a fresh look at Chandler's case. Start over, so to speak. Throw out all our theories and assumptions. Wipe the slate clean and start at square one."

"Good plan. Sort of like those leftovers you shove further and further back in the fridge."

He laughed. "Good analogy."

"I mean do you really think they're going to get better if you push them further back?" She rolled her eyes.

"Okay, I'll throw them out. So, can you get things organized and I'll plan to tackle Chandler's case first thing in the morning? I'm going to take Gus for a quick walk, and then I'll see you at dinner. We'll see what the super sleuths uncovered today."

"Will do," she said with a laugh.

* * *

Coop and Gus got in a walk at the park before the afternoon light dissolved into dusk. The act of walking and playing with Gus spawned a stream of ideas. He was certain a fresh look at the case would nudge a clue loose and lead to progress. The weather forecasters had promised a storm would blow in tonight and Coop felt a damp chill in the air when they returned to the Jeep.

He helped Mrs. Henderson with dinner and volunteered to pick up Chandler since Camille and Charlie had spent the whole afternoon at the center. By the time he returned with Chandler, AB had arrived and was chatting with the pair.

Mrs. Henderson got things on the table while Camille gushed with excitement about their day. "Everybody at the center was whisperin' and gabbin' about the hubbub yesterday. The board called an emergency meeting and gathered in their big conference room. Technically, they're open to the public, so while I was working, Charlie and a few of the others sat in the audience chairs. The police came and left with computers and files."

The group feasted on another delicious meal, passing glazed ham and homemade applesauce around the table as they chattered on about the embezzlement. Peach cobbler and ice cream awaited them.

Charlie took a few sips of his special tea Mrs. Henderson had taken to making him, only a quarter sweetened. "The big news of the meeting was they took action to suspend the bookkeeper and Ms. Stein until the investigation was complete. In the meantime, two of the board members who are retired volunteered to staff the office. They're going to farm out the accounting needs to a local firm until the matter is settled."

"Some of the folks who use the center are concerned and upset. They don't like the chaos, and the board members are trying to ease their anxiety. They're going to have a public meeting next week. They want to assure everyone the center will stay open. They want to keep things as normal as possible."

Chandler added, "My staff tells me Coop and AB were spot on. They found several account numbers that had been altered in the vendor records. They turned the numbers over to the authorities. From what my staff reported, somebody has been messing with the vendor payments for the last six months. Looks like they would divert payments for one or two vendors each month and then switch them back. My staff is helping the police unravel some of it."

With a grin the size of the slab of cobbler Coop was digging into, he said, "Aunt Camille and Dad, you deserve a toast." He raised his glass of sweet tea. "When you first brought up the center, I wasn't sure about it, but it looks like you two uncovered a real crime. Congratulations."

Chandler raised his glass. "They certainly provided me some much-needed excitement and a fun diversion from my own problems."

Camille flushed at the attention. "We couldn't have done it without you, Chandler. You urged those board members on it and got your people in there to look at the records."

"It's a good thing you pressed the issue," said AB. "Hopefully, they can recover once they oust the employees responsible. The center is such an important facility for the community."

"It's wonderful. I wish we had something like it back home. They're putting in walking trails outside and a bird watching sanctuary. It would be a shame to see it close or cut hours," added Charlie.

"It sounds like the bookkeeper and Ms. Stein are both implicated in any criminal activities," said Coop.

Chandler finished his bite of cobbler and said, "That's my understanding. The bookkeeper did the actual transactions and paid the bills. Ms. Stein signed off on the transaction reports. In fairness, she may not have realized the account numbers had been changed, but she approved all the payments."

"I can't wait to tell the ladies at the club about this. We have a meetin' Friday to finalize our gala preparations. Speaking of that, we've got to get you a tuxedo. Coop already has one." Camille looked at Charlie.

"Tuxedo?" he asked with alarm.

"The gala is a formal affair. This year we're raising money for a program for foster children."

"I'll take a ticket," said AB. "You can be my date, Charlie."

"Well, I can't refuse now," he said with a smile. "I guess that means I'll have to let Camille get me into one of those monkey suits."

"Wonderful, AB. I already had you listed at our table." Camille smiled. "That reminds me, I'm not sure I told you, Coop, but I put you down as a participant."

Coop nodded and then looked confused. "What do you mean participant? Aren't I a guest?"

"Oh, dear, I guess it slipped my mind in the all the excitement. We're organizing a bachelor auction this year. I told the ladies you'd be glad to participate."

Coop's face flushed. He saw his dad snickering and AB staring at the wall, her lips quivering. Even Chandler was on the verge of bursting in his efforts to suppress a laugh. "I. Am. Not. Participating."

"Well, Coop, it's all settled. The programs are already at the printer. It'll be fun, and it's for a good cause."

"Grr, Aunt Camille," he whined. "I can't believe you did this to me. I don't want to parade around in front of a bunch of women."

"There are lots of men volunteering. Doctors, professors, policemen, firemen, bankers, businessmen, and lawyers. You're the only private detective, though," Camille said with a sly smile. Her eyes landed on Chandler. "I wish I would have met you before we decided on the programs. I'll remember you for next year."

Chandler's smirk evaporated, replaced with a look of pure terror. "Oh, I don't think I'd make a very good contestant, or whatever you call them. I don't date."

Camille's lips curved and with a glimmer in her eye said, "That's perfect. You'd meet some eligible ladies."

Coop watched, amused to see his aunt use her charms on a new victim. He scooped another bit of cobbler from his dish. "Just surrender, Chandler. She has a way of winning these things."

Camille giggled as she spooned her last bite. "Now that's the smartest thing I've heard you say tonight."

Coop looked across the table at his aunt. "This is going to be humiliating. Are you sure I couldn't just write you a big check?"

AB poked Coop's shoulder. "Cheer up, Coop. It'll be fun."

"Fun for y'all, not so much for me." He leaned toward her and whispered, "Whatever I have to pay, promise me you'll outbid them."

Chapter 20

AB had taken the time to organize and straighten all the files and reports related to Neil's death. Coop's desire to focus anew on Chandler's case would begin with a fresh eyes approach to the police file. She had placed it on the top of the stack of folders.

Despite a layer of ice outside, Coop arrived early Wednesday morning. He and Gus got fires roaring in both fireplaces before he put a pot of coffee on to brew. He kept his jacket over his "I may be wrong, but I doubt it" shirt, waiting for the warmth to permeate the office.

He opened the original police file and settled in to read it. He checked the police timeline against his reconstruction on the whiteboard. The time the 911 call came in matched his—11:55 a.m. He read through the original team's report and noted the food delivery at 11:35 a.m. Coop checked his timeline and saw the video footage showed Jake arriving at that time. Coop's chart also indicated Jake left at 11:42 a.m. Melissa returned to her desk at 11:44 a.m.

Chandler arrived for lunch at 11:46 a.m. and left the office suite at 11:53 a.m. The times were a match with his findings. The calls for a medical emergency were made, and paramedics arrived at 12:01 p.m. and transported Neil. He was pronounced dead in the emergency room at 2:37 p.m. after all efforts had failed and tests showed there was no surgical solution. The coroner's report indicated a massive subarachnoid hemorrhagic stroke which caused severe bleeding.

The toxicology report that followed several days later pinpointed a high amount of what Chandler later helped identify as CX-232. Once the overdose of the drug was found in his system, the detectives focused on those who had access to the drug. That put the spotlight on Chandler, who had the opportunity and the motive.

Coop read through the autopsy report and the medical records from the hospital. Neil's body was still in storage at the morgue since the case was unsolved and the police hadn't authorized its release. He glanced at the inventory sheet of personal property, noting the hospital included photos of everything. Neil's wallet and contents, shirt, tie, pants, watch, underwear, socks, and shoes. All the items had been seized as evidence once the death was deemed suspicious. His belongings were now in an evidence room.

Gus shot off for the back door and Coop heard AB talking to him about how cold it was outside. Her winter boots made a heavy thud as they hit the floor. He turned his attention back to the report but was interrupted by his cell phone.

"Mr. Harrington, I'm sorry to call so early. It's Melissa from Borlund. Neil's assistant."

"No problem, I'm at work. What can I do for you?"

"I was hoping you could come by Borlund. I'm cleaning out Neil's office and I, uh, well, I found something that you need to see."

Coop frowned and promised to be there within the hour. He found AB standing in front of the fireplace and Gus at her feet.

"Miserable out there," she said. "I think we need a telecommuting policy for days like this."

He grinned. "Well, I'm headed back out in it. Melissa summoned me." He slipped into his jacket and extracted gloves from his pockets. "I'll bring us back a late breakfast or early lunch."

"I'll be here. Madison and Ross are working tonight on that surveillance job. I feel for them. They're going to freeze."

Gus didn't even get up to follow Coop. He was more than happy to stay with AB in front of the warm fire, getting his neck rubbed.

Coop took it slow on the slick roads and checked in with security before proceeding upstairs to Neil's old office suite. He found Melissa at her desk; the color drained from her face.

"Are you okay?"

"I...I don't know. See for yourself and see what you think." She led the way to Neil's office.

Several boxes were strewn across the floor and on the couch and conference table. She had been boxing up his personal possessions and sorting through things. She led him to the conference table and pointed at a suit jacket. "He kept a few shirts and a spare suit here. I was boxing these for pickup by one of the charities. His family asked me to donate the clothes."

She touched the fabric. "This was the jacket he wore that day. The day he died. He usually always removed it for lunch, and it was still hanging in the closet. I never even thought about it until today."

Coop looked at the jacket. "Okaaay, so what did you find?"

"Well, I was going through the pockets, just to make sure they were empty. I put it back when I realized what it was." She opened the top of the pocket and urged Coop to look inside.

He took a peek and saw a small syringe. "Neil wasn't diabetic, was he?"

She shook her head. "No, I'm not sure what he'd be doing with a syringe."

Coop didn't want to touch it and left it in the pocket. He pulled out his cell and put in a call to Ben to get an evidence tech dispatched.

Minutes later, Jimmy and Kate strode through the door with a technician. They took Melissa's statement, and the technician collected her fingerprints. He bagged the syringe and the jacket and wrote a receipt for Melissa.

Kate and Jimmy asked Melissa to suspend her packing and attached crime scene tape across the doors. They directed her to keep it locked and attached an evidence seal across the joint where the two doors met.

They thanked Melissa and Coop promised to be in touch as he left with the two detectives.

"We'll put a rush on it and get it analyzed for residue and prints," said Kate. "We'll give you a call when we know anything."

Coop saw the weather hadn't improved and elected to swing by the cafeteria and pick up breakfast rather than slide through the streets to a restaurant. He detoured to a men's room down the hall to wash his hands.

He waved a hello to Bernie, who was escorting a couple of maintenance technicians to a locked door in the hallway. "Hey, Bernie, how ya doing?"

"Sick of the cold weather." He took out a key and opened the door. "Talk to you later, Coop. Gotta get these two access to some kitchen equipment."

"No problem. See ya later." Coop retrieved two boxes from the cafeteria and headed back to the office.

When Coop arrived, he put the takeout containers on the kitchen table and hollered at AB. Gus came running through the door, his nose leading him to the possibility of food. AB followed a few minutes later.

He unpacked their veggie scrambles and bacon. "Coop, your shoes, they're tracking mud all over. You need to take them off."

He looked down and muttered. "I forgot. What a mess." He took delicate steps to the back door and deposited his grimy boots on the mat before slipping on his loafers. The action caused an idea to burst in his mind.

He hustled to his office, bypassing the breakfast table. He grabbed the report on Neil and rushed back to the kitchen. Gus, assuming it was a game, chased after him and slid along the wooden floor.

"What in the devil are you doing?" asked AB.

"I was in the middle of reviewing this medical report and autopsy when Melissa called. I was just starting to look at the photos of Neil's personal effects. The hospital takes them, probably to minimize fraudulent claims." He turned the page to the photos and showed them to AB. "Anyway, check out Neil's shoes."

She studied the report. "Definitely a tasseled wingtip."

He went on to tell her about the syringe Melissa found. "Could it be that Neil's our guy?"

She frowned and said, "What? Are you saying the syringe Melissa found was the one used to doctor the soup?"

Coop nodded and said "See where this is going?"

She said, "So, Neil put the drug in the soup thinking it was Chandler's."

"Because it was on the serving cart with Chandler's nametag. Then Marco saw the mistake with the cilantro and switched the bowls."

AB paused and contemplated Coop's theory. "Neil wanted to kill Chandler and ended up eating the soup with the lethal dose by mistake."

Between bites, Coop said, "I think that's exactly what happened. Chandler wouldn't budge on selling. Neil needed the money. He had access to the lab." He took a bite of toast. "I need to go back and look at the camera footage and take a closer look at Neil's movements that day."

AB offered to clear away the breakfast dishes, and Gus positioned himself near the sink, knowing AB would cave and give him a bite of her eggs. When she had tidied the area, she fixed a cup of tea and joined Coop in his office.

Coop stared at his screen. "Okay, so I saw in the logs where Neil arrived on that day just before eight. He used his office elevator from the ground floor to his office at twenty after eleven. I was searching around the hallway that goes to his elevator and I don't see him. I was trying to figure out where he came from and if he visited the kitchen.

AB stood behind Coop and watched as he scrolled through footage. He murmured his impressions as he viewed the screen. "Bernie said there are no cameras in the stairwells. Maybe he used a stairwell. The priority for coverage is the entry points. I remember seeing a camera in the main hallway outside the cafeteria. I would think he would show up on that one."

After hours of viewing, Coop had no luck spotting Neil on any of the cameras in the building. "That's strange in itself," said AB.

"Like he dodged them on purpose?"

She nodded. "That's what I'm thinking."

Coop picked up the phone and put in a call to Bernie. "Sorry to bother you again, but I have a quick question. I saw you unlocking the door near the private elevator area today, and you mentioned kitchen equipment. Where does that door lead?"

"Oh, that's the service corridor. It runs behind the kitchen, and we use it for contractor access for maintenance. Things like pumping the grease traps and dealing with mechanical issues. That way they don't have to run through the main cafeteria or kitchen."

"Is there access to the break room from there?"

"Yeah, you can get to the break room from that hall."

"Is it possible to get me a list of people with keys to that door?"

"Sure, I'll send you a copy over right away. It's limited, so it won't be a long list."

Coop thanked him and disconnected. "I think I know where Neil went on his stealth mission."

"Unbelievable." She shuddered. "If Neil is our killer, I guess justice will be served."

"It's a theory at this point. I need to prove it."

He saw the email come through from Bernie. He read it and pushed the print button and handed AB a copy.

"So, all the security personnel have a key, Arlo, his assistant chefs, Neil, Chandler, Melissa, and Amanda."

"Small list," said AB. "We've eliminated the kitchen staff, Melissa and Amanda were seen on camera, and it was a man's shoe. That leaves Chandler and Neil."

"And only one of them had a syringe in his jacket pocket that day." Coop looked at his watch. "I was hoping they'd have the results from that by now."

"When is Chandler going back to work?"

"Tomorrow is his plan. He had a follow-up appointment today, and if all goes well, he'll start back with at least partial days tomorrow. He'll have to see how he feels, but he's going stir crazy at the house."

"He hasn't had any security issues at his house since he put in the new system, right?"

Coop nodded. "Yeah. The car running him down was the only threat. I'm beginning to think that was just an accident and the driver may not have even known Chandler was hurt or fell. Could have just been an overreaction due to Chandler's knowledge that he was the target."

"He may have gotten scared and then tripped and fell, imagining the driver was after him."

Coop hit the button for Ben and explained the current theory. He reasoned Neil's shoes, the syringe, and the access he had to the hallway in the kitchen were as compelling as the evidence they had used against Chandler.

They talked for a few minutes and Coop disconnected. "He says it sounds like a plausible explanation. He wants the techs to dig into the video footage and see if they can do any better than we did. He's going to have them examine Neil's shoes, and he'll call us with the lab results on the syringe tomorrow morning."

"I think we're onto something. It explains everything and the reason we couldn't pin it on any of the doctors on the team. Neil had access, but we didn't consider him because he was the victim."

Coop nodded. "Exactly. Talk about dead wrong." He gave her a mischievous grin and said, "Come over to Aunt Camille's for dinner. We can celebrate our progress. She'd be thrilled to have you."

"Sounds good. I'm getting hungry, and Mrs. Henderson's cooking beats mine, hands down."

"Let's pack it up for the night. I'll give Chandler a call when I get home and give him an update on the investigation and the evidence that points to Neil being his own killer."

Chapter 21

The smell of fresh cinnamon rolls greeted Coop the next morning. He couldn't resist the temptation and snagged one from the pan where Mrs. Henderson had left them to cool. He poured himself a cup of coffee and spread the newspaper on the counter. Gus sat at attention, watching every bite Coop ate.

He saw the Heritage Center article at the bottom of the first page. Aunt Camille's meddling had led to the arrest of the bookkeeper at the center. Ms. Stein had been fired, but not charged. According to the reporter, the bookkeeper had been manipulating electronic payments for several vendors over the last nine months. Instead of paying vendors she had been directing the funds to her own personal accounts.

A spokesperson for the board indicated they would be pressing for restitution to recoup over one hundred thousand dollars that had been siphoned off in the scheme. They would be working to find the funds to pay the outstanding debts owed to the vendors who had never been paid. Several of the board members were making personal donations to the center, and they had established an account to collect public donations.

Coop slipped Gus a tiny bite of his breakfast and turned when he heard Charlie making his way into the kitchen. "Check it out, Dad. You guys made the front page." He poured his dad a cup of coffee and slid the paper to him.

Charlie put on his reading glasses and read the article. "Wow, that's a lot of money she stole. Good thing your aunt did something. It could have been worse."

"You two make quite the pair of detectives. They didn't name you in the article; just said two seniors who were suspicious were instrumental in uncovering the crime."

"Your aunt will be pleased," said Charlie, eyeing the pan of cinnamon rolls. "Those smell delicious." Coop plucked one from the pan and put it on a plate.

"Enjoy your success. Tell Aunt Camille congratulations. I've got to get to the office. We've got a break in Chandler's case." Coop stole another cinnamon roll for AB and slipped it into a plastic container. He hollered, "See you tonight, Dad," as he and Gus left for the day.

As soon as Coop sat down at his desk, Chandler called. "Hey, Coop, I've been going through some of the mail Amanda held for me. I just opened a set of documents addressed to Neil. They were sent by a lawyer in California. The letter says he's sorry to hear about the death of his partner and that he has drawn up the documents as Neil requested to remove me from the corporation. He indicated a death certificate would be necessary. He also included documents Neil would need to sign to sell the business to FuturePharma in New York. He said the corporate change would have to take place first and then the sale could proceed with Neil's signature alone."

Chandler's voice went up an octave. "The attorney references a conversation the two of them had the morning of Neil's death." He paused and said, "This is too weird. I had a hard time grasping what you were telling me last night, but now this…"

"Could you send me a copy of those documents? I'll give the attorney a call and see what I can learn."

Coop sent Ben a text to keep him in the loop with the latest revelation. He drummed his fingers on his desk while he waited for the email from Chandler. As soon as he saw it, he printed it out and scanned through the information.

He located the phone number of the attorney from Menlo Park, California. He looked at the clock, hoping the firm opened at eight o'clock. He put in a call and was connected to Mr. Slade, the attorney who wrote the letter. Coop explained he was investigating the death of Neil Borden from Borlund Sciences and that his assistant had just opened the documents he had sent Neil. He provided Ben's name and phone number should he need a reference.

"I'm confused, Mr. Harrington. You must mean Mr. Hollund's death. He's the partner Neil said died."

"No, I'm working on Neil's case. I'm sorry to say Neil died the afternoon he talked with you about preparing the documents."

"Oh, my. How horrible. Both partners died? That's unbelievable."

Coop didn't correct him. "I'm hoping to get a little information from you."

"Of course. I'll do whatever I can to help."

"How did you know Neil?"

"I didn't know him. He was referred to me by another client of mine. Derrick Hudson. Mr. Borden said he worked with Derrick in the past out here in California. Derrick suggested he use me as I've done a lot of corporate work for pharmaceutical companies."

"I see. Did Neil indicate why he didn't want to use a local attorney here in Nashville?"

"Not in so many words. Neil gave me the impression he wanted to keep things confidential and didn't want to alarm the employees about the upcoming sale of the company. I do all the acquisition paperwork for Mr. Hudson's company, and he was confident I could handle this for Mr. Borden."

"That makes sense."

Mr. Slade sighed and said, "May I ask how Mr. Borden died?"

"He had a massive stroke."

"That's mindboggling. Neil told me his partner, Mr. Hollund, collapsed at work and they thought it was a stroke."

"Well, I appreciate your time. Neil's death has been ruled a homicide. I'll be giving your information to the detectives working the case, and they may be calling you if they need anything else."

"Oh my, he was murdered? Do they have any suspects?"

"We're working on a couple of leads. You've been a great help." Coop took down Mr. Slade's cell number and thanked him before ending the conversation.

AB came through the door with raised brows and saw Coop grinning. "I take it you've had another breakthrough?"

With a lilt in his voice Coop related his conversation with the attorney. "I think we need to burrow further into Derrick Hudson's life."

She pulled his file from those on the conference table. "His and Neil's paths crossed at school and the company they worked for in California. I'll see what I can find out about that company." She tapped her finger on the report. "I noted in here it was bought out in 2004."

"I'm going to get Ben moving on this and see what he can do."

* * *

Ben arrived at Harrington and Associates at noon. He joined Coop and AB at the conference table in Coop's office. "So, we got the results on the syringe. There was CX-232 in it. Only Neil's prints and Melissa's were on it."

Ben shook his head. "We never considered he was the killer. Now that we're looking at things from that angle, it's making sense. His shoes are a good match for the image from the kitchen."

"Anything on Derrick Hudson?" asked Coop.

"As a matter of fact, yes. On a longshot, Kate took an extended look at his credit card history. We had been working on that burner phone number Neil had been calling off and on. We found out both phones were purchased at a drugstore in Washington last year."

"And you found the purchase on Hudson's card?" asked Coop.

"We did indeed. We discovered a purchase at that drugstore and just got the confirming receipt for the two prepaid cell phones. Hudson must have mailed one to Neil."

"I wonder if Mr. Hudson has a secret bank account in the Caymans?" asked Coop.

"We called Treasury today and have somebody working on that angle. If he has one, he's careful. There are no transfers to or from his other bank accounts. Kate and Jimmy have been combing through his finances."

"How about we bluff him a little?" suggested Coop.

They listened with interest as Coop explained his strategy.

* * *

Later that afternoon, Coop and AB left Gus on his bed in Ben's office while they gathered in a conference room. The room was outfitted with multiple flat-screen monitors and state of the art audio and video equipment. Ben was sitting at the table watching the screen where Kate and Jimmy could be viewed. They were connected via a video conference system to authorities in California.

Kate and Jimmy had spent the last few hours setting up a joint interview with local officials who were bringing Derrick in for questioning. Coop gave Ben a questioning look.

"We're not live, just observing in here. We can talk to Kate or Jimmy, but not the other end."

"Any word from Treasury?"

He shook his head. "Not yet."

Coop and AB slipped into chairs and watched the other screen fill with activity. Coop recognized the man ushered into the room between the two detectives. "That's him."

Ben said, "They said he was cooperative and agreed to come in and answer questions related to the investigation into Neil's death."

The detectives thanked Derrick, offered him coffee or water and provided a written document for his signature. It outlined his Miranda rights and his agreement to the interview by the local authorities and the Nashville detectives via video conference. The detectives with Derrick emphasized the reason for the document was the video questioning by an outside agency.

Derrick asked about the Miranda warning in the text, and the detectives told him it was standard operating procedure. He shrugged and signed the paper, and the detectives added their signatures.

The local detectives began the interview verifying Derrick's name, date of birth, address, and place of employment. They then introduced Kate and Jimmy as detectives with the Nashville Police Department.

Jimmy began the interview and went over much of the same ground Coop had covered in his conversation with Derrick. Kate took over and said, "Mr. Hudson, we've uncovered new information that implicates you in the attempted murder of Neil's partner, Chandler Hollund."

"What? What do you mean?"

"Did you buy a prepaid cell phone from a drugstore in Woodinville, Washington, on September 9, 2015?"

"What? I have no idea."

"Were you in Washington on that date?"

"I can't remember that long ago."

Kate pulled a piece of paper from the file and said, "Item number one." She waited while the detective in California placed a copy of the document in front of Derrick. "This is your credit card statement from September 2015. It shows several charges in Woodinville and the surrounding area. The highlighted charge is for two prepaid cell phones. Do you deny you made the charge?"

Derrick stared at the paper. "Uh, yeah, I remember. I was in Washington for a conference. My cell phone was messed up, so I had to buy a prepaid to get by."

"You had to buy two of them?" she asked. "The phone records from those phones show calls made between you and Neil Borden." Her eyes bore into the camera. "Can you explain why you bought a prepaid phone for Neil Borlund?" The detectives slid another sheet of paper, illustrating the call histories, in front of Derrick.

Derrick stammered. "I probably loaned it to him at a conference or something."

"Right," said Kate. "We uncovered a document on Neil's computer. He implicated you as the one who forced him to kill Chandler. Chandler wouldn't sell the company, and Neil needed the money to pay you."

"That's crazy," he yelled. "I didn't tell Neil to kill Chandler. I had nothing to do with that."

"Did you refer Neil to Mr. Slade, the attorney you use for your corporate acquisitions?" asked Kate.

Derrick nodded. "So, what if I did?"

"I'll take that as a yes. Mr. Slade has already provided us that information." Her voice was firm and methodical. "Neil contacted Mr. Slade the morning he planned to kill Chandler. He wanted the paperwork done in a rush and wanted it kept quiet. Selling the company was the only way to get you the money you demanded."

She flipped through her file. "Neil outlined the bribery scheme you set up, and we have his bank records showing huge sums of money transferred to your account in the Cayman Islands. We're prepared to charge you with the attempted murder of Chandler Hollund."

"Wait a minute. I told you I didn't have anything to do with any murder."

"Is that right? Do you deny receiving money from Neil via your account in the Cayman Islands?"

He hung his head.

"We've spoken with the District Attorney. We've arranged to extradite you back to Nashville for the attempted murder charge. We have Neil's own words to implicate you. And then there's his death," said Jimmy.

"There may be an opportunity for you, Mr. Hudson," said Kate. "Tell us more about your financial dealings with Neil and the Cayman Islands accounts, and we'd be willing to advocate on your behalf with the District Attorney."

He shook his head. "I'll be in a real mess with the Internal Revenue Service with my account in the Caymans."

Kate interrupted. "We don't care about your taxes and the money you're hiding. We need your side of the bribery story if we're going to go to bat for you with the DA. So, tell us now. We have officers at the airport ready to fly out to San Francisco and bring you back here."

"Oh, man. Number one, I never suggested murder or had anything to do with the murder. All I did was help out Neil years ago, and he was paying me back."

"So you loaned him more than four hundred thousand dollars?"

"Neil made a mistake back at our old company. He embezzled, and I covered it for him."

"This was back at NewGen Pharmaceuticals?" asked Jimmy.

"Right. Neil stole over a hundred thousand dollars. They agreed not to turn the matter over to the police if he left quietly and paid the money back. He didn't have the money, so I covered it for him. He agreed to pay me back each month."

Kate looked at her file. "So, he paid you two thousand a month for about ten years. That's well over a hundred thousand dollars."

"Interest," said Derrick.

"Things changed in 2015, around the time you started communicating with Neil using the burner phones."

"Yeah, well, we came to a new understanding. A new payment plan. He was way more successful than I was. His success was due to my silence."

"So you upped the amount in exchange for keeping his past indiscretions quiet?" asked Kate.

"Right. Right. It was a business arrangement. He was willing to pay anything so as not to jeopardize his company. He and Chandler were hot in the biz. Chandler's one of the best. Everyone knew they would make millions with this new Alzheimer's drug."

"And you just wanted your cut for playing a role in his success. I can see that," said Jimmy, giving the nod to the camera.

Kate looked at her notes again. "So you raised your monthly price to five thousand and then about four months ago there was another price increase to twenty thousand. Is that accurate?"

Derrick squinted and said, "Yeah, that sounds right."

"Neil also routed a large payment to you for close to one hundred thousand dollars in November when he sold his house, correct?"

He snickered. "Sort of like an early Christmas bonus. Yeah, that's right."

"And you were demanding how much more money now?" asked Kate.

"Neil negotiated a buyout. He was going to pay me ten million dollars, and I promised our business would be concluded. He'd never hear from me again."

"I've got copies of your account statement here," Kate said, her voice steady. She read off a series of numbers to verify his account. This was the riskiest bluff of the interrogation.

"No, no," he said and corrected her on the number sequence.

"Sorry, my mistake. I grabbed Neil's instead of yours."

Ben picked up the phone and placed a call. He recited the account number Derrick had given. "You'll need to hurry it up. We're about done with the interview."

He hung up the phone and shook his head with disgust. "Feds. Either they're in the way when you don't want them or not there when you need them."

Kate and Jimmy were slow rolling the rest of the conversation. They summarized the bribery scheme again. They probed the attempted murder with relentless questioning. They asked about Derrick's knowledge of CX-232. They bought some time and asked him about his association with all the scientists on Chandler's team. They asked if he suggested Neil poison Chandler.

"I never did such a thing. I told Neil he needed to convince Chandler to sell. To do whatever he had to do to get that sale done. Then we could conclude our arrangement."

"All you did was apply so much pressure that Neil believed he had no other choice." Kate's voice did little to hide her contempt for the man sitting across the country staring at her.

The detectives in California had Derrick complete a written statement outlining the bribery arrangement with Neil. As he was finishing his account, the phone in the conference room rang.

Ben picked it up and said, "Ok, good. I'll let them know." Ben disconnected and punched in the extension for Kate's conference room.

"Treasury has two guys outside the room Derrick is in out there. They're ready once we're done. I think we have what we need for the bribery portion."

Coop watched Kate nod and heard her say "Got it."

Derrick shoved the paper across the table and said, "Okay, so now you have this information. You'll get the DA to forget this attempted murder nonsense."

"That's right. We'll be dropping the pursuit of charges related to the attempted murder of Chandler Hollund."

"Okay, so I'm free to go?"

"We've got everything we need," said Kate with a nod.

The detective in California opened the door, and as Derrick turned around, two men in dark suits came through the door. One of them removed his credentials and said, "I'm Special Agent Sharp. Derrick Hudson, you're under arrest for violation of the Foreign Account Tax Compliance Act and violation of the Hobb's Act in your use of interstate commerce to commit acts of bribery."

Derrick turned back around and faced the camera. "You told me you didn't care about the money in the Caymans."

Kate smiled. "I told you *we* didn't care about your account. It turns out the FBI and the US Treasury do care."

He began yelling at the camera. His face and neck bloomed with red blotches as his voice rose. He bellowed another expletive and Ben cut the audio feed to the conference room.

Ben muttered, "What a Class-A jerk."

Coop smiled at Ben. "We got a slice of justice. Mr. Hudson should be stripped of his wealth and probably end up spending a few years behind bars for the federal crimes."

Ben said, "Yeah. I'm glad to get this one closed."

Coop smiled at AB. "We'll swing by and give Chandler the good news. Poor guy's been living with this hanging over him for far too long."

"The DA elected to let the Feds have Derrick. The penalties for interstate crime are far harsher than anything he would get here for bribery. Not to mention with Neil being dead, it would be tough to prosecute."

AB said, "I know Neil intended to kill Chandler, but a part of me feels sorry for him. I know he made horrible choices, but this clown," she pointed to the monitor on the wall, "is repulsive."

Coop nodded. "Derrick is despicable, but Neil's desire for money got the best of him. He paid the ultimate price for his greed. I'm glad he didn't succeed with his plan that day. The world needs more Chandlers and less Neils in my book."

Chapter 22

Coop and AB collected Gus and made their way to Borlund. They checked in with Bernie's office, and he escorted them upstairs to Chandler's suite. Coop introduced AB to Amanda and said, "We're here to see Chandler. Tell him I've got good news."

Amanda smiled and rang into the lab. "He'll be right here."

"So you solved the case?" asked Bernie.

"We did, with the help of the police."

They heard Chandler coming down the hall with his distinctive hobble. His ankle had improved, but he was using a cane when he walked. "Hey, Amanda says there's good news?"

"Do you want to go into your office?" asked Coop.

"Yeah, I need to sit down" He motioned to Bernie and Amanda, "You two come join us. We could all use some good news."

When they had gathered around the conference table, Coop explained how all the evidence pointed to Neil plotting to poison Chandler to gain control of the company. "He was desperate for money because he was being blackmailed by a former colleague from California. The guy was increasing his demands and pressure."

Coop further described the embezzlement from years ago and Derrick's offer to help Neil, which had turned into years of pressure and hundreds of thousands of dollars funneled to a secret account in the Cayman Islands. "Neil was going to pay him ten million dollars with the understanding that he would go away and never be heard from again."

"I doubt that would have worked," said Chandler. "He probably would have kept coming after him."

"I wouldn't have trusted him," said Coop. "But, that's what he was planning on doing with some of the proceeds from the sale of the company. I'm sure Neil intended to take the rest and disappear."

Bernie nodded. "So, if the kitchen hadn't switched the soups, Chandler would have been the victim?"

Coop nodded. "Right. Neil's plan backfired because he didn't know the difference between parsley and cilantro. Without that mistake, Chandler would have most likely died, and Neil's scheme would have worked."

Amanda turned to her boss. "I can't believe he was willing to kill you."

"I wish he would have told me about his situation. I would have gladly given him the money to pay off this guy."

Coop's forehead wrinkled. "I think Neil knew Derrick would just keep upping the ante. He would have demanded more and more. He'd already done that to Neil. I suppose that's part of the reason he wanted to sell. He could walk away with the money, and there would be no more threat because he wouldn't have to work again."

Chandler's shoulders sagged and he exhaled. "This is surreal. I've been struggling to believe Neil would kill me. It's not a comfortable feeling." He moved his hand and knocked his cane to the floor. Coop bent and retrieved it for him.

Bernie stood and extended his hand to Chandler. "Dr. Hollund, I'm just glad you're back. You can put this behind you now. Things will get back to normal. We're all with you."

Amanda nodded and said, "Nobody thought you did it. Bernie's right, it'll be good to put an end to all the intrigue and speculation around here. How about I arrange for a staff meeting tomorrow morning? You can make the announcement."

Chandler thought for a few moments and said, "That's a great idea. It's better they hear it from me and ask their questions so we can get back to business."

She stood and excused herself to organize the meeting. Bernie clasped Coop on the shoulder and said, "It's been a pleasure, Coop. Stop by sometime, and I'll treat you to lunch." He gave him a wink and a handshake.

The door closed behind the two and Coop turned to Chandler. "How are ya managing?"

"Still a little shocked, but at least we have answers. I need to focus on moving forward and figure out what I'm going to do here. The possibility of my looming arrest has sort of paralyzed me. Not to mention the accident." He pointed at his ankle.

"Ben said he talked to the DA and confirmed all pending charges against you have been dropped. We think your fall and the car you saw speeding by had nothing to do with the case. It was an unfortunate coincidence, probably magnified by our focus on figuring out who was targeting you," said Coop.

Chandler nodded. "Yeah, I realized that yesterday. I feel like a complete idiot."

"You're far from an idiot. You're one of the smartest guys I've ever met. You just need to get back in your zone and focus on your research," said Coop, patting his shoulder.

"I've got to find someone to manage the business side of this place."

"I have a thought for you on that front. I've got a client who has a large accounting firm here in Nashville with offices in Atlanta and Raleigh. How about we set up a meeting and see if they can find you someone trustworthy to be your business manager? As you said, you don't need a partner, just a good business manager who knows the industry."

Chandler's eyes brightened. "That sounds like a terrific idea. I've been dreading the whole thing, but need somebody in that position. We've got some great staff members who are keeping things running, but I need someone with experience."

AB smiled and said, "I'll give them a call when we get back to the office and set something up for next week."

"Sounds good. I appreciate the help." Chandler added, "Not just with the case. Spending time with the two of you and your family, Coop, inspired me. I decided I need to make time to visit my family. My parents aren't getting any younger, and my work has consumed me for longer than I care to admit. I want to get this place back on track, and the trials started on CX-232, and then I'm going to take a vacation. I want to spend time with my family before I start the new project. I'm hoping to convince them to come out here later in the year and spend a month. This ordeal has given a whole new meaning to the idea of life being too short."

"That's wonderful, Chandler. I'm glad to see something positive for you come out of this tough situation." Coop looked at his watch. "We should get going; it's almost closing time."

Chandler stood and extended his hand to both of them. "I can't begin to thank you for everything you've done."

Coop shook his hand and put an arm around his shoulder. "I'm just sorry we didn't figure it out sooner. This was a weird one."

AB hugged him and said, "Don't be a stranger, Chandler. Stop by and see us sometime. We'll see you at the gala in a couple of weeks, right?" She gave him a wink and grinned at Coop.

With a shy smile, he said, "I wouldn't miss it and I will. I mean it. I'll stop by or give you a call and maybe we can all go to dinner one night, my treat."

"We never refuse a free meal," said Coop with a chuckle.

Chandler moved to his desk and said, "Hang on just a minute." He opened a drawer and scribbled out a check. "I want you to have this. Consider it a heartfelt thank you, a bonus for all you did for me. "

Coop shook his head. "That's not necessary. We were just doing our jobs."

"I insist." Chandler pushed the check closer to Coop. "You never gave up. That means a lot to me. I'll never forget it. Please, it would make me happy."

Coop took the check and stuffed it in his pocket. "Thank you." AB hugged Chandler again.

They said goodbye to Amanda when they walked by her desk and made for the elevator. Coop punched the button and said, "Aunt Camille is expecting you for dinner. She and Dad want all the details of the case."

AB grinned as they left the building. "I'd expect nothing less. Not to mention the fun we'll have needling you about your debut appearance at her bachelor auction."

"Remember what I made you promise me. Any amount of money."

She wiggled her brows. "Any?"

Coop patted his pocket where he had tucked Chandler's check. "Trust me, we can afford it."

ACKNOWLEDGEMENTS

I have so much fun spending time with Coop and all the characters in these mysteries. Like all books, this one started with a weird *what if* question. In case you're a reader who likes to read the end of the book first, I won't give anything away, so I'll leave it at that. Suffice it to say, I worked to concoct a mystery with a twist, one I hope you enjoyed.

Each of the Cooper Harrington novels reveals a bit more about Coop's background, and in *Dead Wrong* you get a healthy dose of Coop's mother. She's wreaking havoc and causing Coop all sorts of trouble. You also get an introduction to Coop's dad, Charlie.

My early readers are always willing to critique my work and provide such useful feedback for improvements. I'm grateful for Theresa, Vicki, Linda, Lorri, and Dana, who were kind enough to read drafts. I always have fun concocting ideas with my dad, who is my number one resource for all things related to crimes, being in law enforcement for over thirty years.

Keri at Alchemy Book Covers and Designs does an excellent job and is the consummate professional when it comes to cover design. Jason and Marina at Polgarus deliver expert formatting and are always pleasant and accommodating.

I'm grateful for the support and encouragement of my friends and family as I continue to pursue my dream of writing. I appreciate all of the readers who have taken the time to provide a review on Amazon. These reviews are especially important in promoting future books, so if you enjoy my novels, please consider leaving a positive review. Follow this link to my author page and select a book to leave your review at www.amazon.com/author/tammylgrace. I also encourage you to follow me on Amazon and you'll be the first to know about new releases.

Remember to visit my website at http://www.tammylgrace.com/contact-tammy.html and join my exclusive group of readers. Follow me on Facebook at www.facebook.com/tammylgrace.books and keep in touch—I'd love to hear from you.

From the Author

Thank you for reading the third book in the Cooper Harrington Detective Novels. This series can be read as stand-alone novels, but I recommend reading them in order, as you'll learn and understand more about the characters as their backgrounds are revealed in subsequent novels. If you enjoy the series and are a fan of women's fiction, you'll want to try my Hometown Harbor Series, filled with the complex relationships of friendship and family. Set in the picturesque San Juan Islands in Washington, you'll escape with a close-knit group of friends and their interwoven lives filled with both challenges and joys. Each book in the series focuses on a different woman and her journey of self-discovery. Be sure and download the free novella, HOMETOWN HARBOR: THE BEGINNING. It's a prequel to FINDING HOME that I know you'll enjoy.

I'd love to send you my exclusive interview with the canine companions in the Hometown Harbor Series as a thank-you for joining my exclusive group of readers. Instructions and a link for signing up for my mailing list are included below. You'll also find questions for book club discussions at www.tammylgrace.com.

Enjoy this book?
You can make a big difference

Thanks again for reading my work and if you enjoy my novels, *I would be grateful if you would leave a review on Amazon*. Authors need reviews to help showcase their work and market it across other platforms. I'd like to be able to take out full-page ads in the newspaper, but I don't have the financial muscle of a big New York publisher. When it comes to getting attention for my work, reviews are some of the most powerful tools I have. You can help by sharing what you enjoyed with other readers.

If you enjoyed my books, please consider leaving a review

Hometown Harbor: The Beginning (FREE Prequel Novella)
Finding Home (Book 1)
Home Blooms (Book 2)
A Promise of Home (Book 3)
Pieces of Home (Book 4)
Finally Home (Book 5)
Killer Music: A Cooper Harrington Detective Novel (Book 1)
Deadly Connection: A Cooper Harrington Detective Novel (Book 2)
Dead Wrong: A Cooper Harrington Detective Novel (Book 3)

Thank you very much for taking the time to leave a review.

ABOUT THE AUTHOR

Tammy L. Grace is the award-winning author of the Cooper Harrington Detective Novels and the Hometown Harbor Series. You'll find Tammy online at www.tammylgrace.com where you can join her mailing list and be part of her exclusive group of readers. Connect with Tammy on Facebook at www.facebook.com/tammylgrace.books or on Twitter at @TammyLGrace.

Made in the USA
Lexington, KY
14 May 2019